# "He's A Mess, Mom," He Heard A Voice Say.

Noah couldn't have agreed more. His head was splitting, and his mouth tasted as if someone had served him scrambled socks. He opened an eye to find a saucy-eyed six-year-old—and her mother, with her bright green eyes and flashing red hair—standing at the foot of his bed.

"It's your alarm clock calling," she said brightly. "You need to get up."

"Can you talk a little more quietly?" Noah burrowed more deeply into his pillow.

"You ignore me when I talk more quietly," she told him. "Do you remember last night? You got my ranch hands drunk. And we have to brand a couple of hundred cattle this morning."

He recognized that tone of voice. "Ms. McCann, don't you realize *you* work for *me?*"

She ignored him. "Mr. Campbell, do you ride?"

"Oh, yes. I ride."

He would ride today, all right, even if it killed him.

Dear Reader,

Welcome to Silhouette Desire, where you can discover the answers to *all* your romantic questions. Such as...

Q. *What would you think if you discovered the man you love has a secret identity—as a movie star?*

A. That's what happens to the heroine of August's MAN OF THE MONTH, *Don't Fence Me In* by award-winning writer Kathleen Korbel.

Q. *What would you do if you were pregnant, in labor and snowbound with a sexy—but panicked—stranger?*

A. Discover the answer in *Father on the Brink,* the conclusion to Elizabeth Bevarly's FROM HERE TO PATERNITY series.

Q. *Suppose you had to have a marriage of convenience?*

A. Maybe you'd behave like the heroine in Barbara McMahon's *Bride of a Thousand Days.*

Q. *How could you talk a man into fathering your child...no strings attached?*

A. Learn how in Susan Crosby's *Baby Fever!*

Q. *Would you ever marry a stranger?*

A. You might, if he was the hero of Sara Orwig's *The Bride's Choice.*

Q. *What does it take to lasso a sexy cowboy?*

A. Find out in Shawna Delacorte's *Cowboy Dreaming.*

Silhouette Desire...where all your questions are answered and your romantic dreams can come true.

Until next month, happy reading!

*Lucia Macro*

Senior Editor

Please address questions and book requests to:
Silhouette Reader Service
U.S.: 3010 Walden Ave., P.O. Box 1325, Buffalo, NY 14269
Canadian: P.O. Box 609, Fort Erie, Ont. L2A 5X3

# KATHLEEN KORBEL
## DON'T FENCE ME IN

SILHOUETTE *Desire*
Published by Silhouette Books
**America's Publisher of Contemporary Romance**

Thanks to my Internet buddies for the help on
Montana: Karen Steens, Laura Ann Anderson and
Miriam Pace. You guys are great.

 SILHOUETTE BOOKS

ISBN 0-373-76015-9

DON'T FENCE ME IN

This edition published by arrangement with Harlequin Books S.A.

® and TM are trademarks of Harlequin Books S.A., used under license.
Trademarks indicated with ® are registered in the United States Patent
and Trademark Office, the Canadian Trade Marks Office and in other
countries.

Printed in U.S.A.

## KATHLEEN KORBEL

lives in St. Louis with her husband and two children. She devotes her time to enjoying her family, writing, avoiding anyone who tries to explain the intricacies of the computer and searching for the fabled house-cleaning fairies. She's had her best luck with her writing—from which she's garnered a *Romantic Times* award for Best New Category Author of 1987, the 1990 Romance Writers of America RITA Award for Best Romantic Suspense and the 1990, 1992 and 1995 RITA awards for Best Long Category Romance—and with her family, without whom she couldn't have managed any of the rest. She hasn't given up on those fairies, though.

"Listen, he's no Clark Gable at home."
                                    —Carole Lombard

# Prologue

He was magic. Even before the crowd caught its first glimpse of his patent-leather-shod foot swing out the open door of the limo, it held its breath in anticipation. Even before they heard the already legendary voice, they sighed. Leaned forward. Focused their entire attention right past the reigning macho hero and his giggly, buxom date to witness the appearance of the man every one of them had actually come to see.

A leg. An arm. A slow unfolding of over six feet of honed, elegant male.

The whispers grew. The sighs built. The flashes multiplied like an approaching electrical storm. And then, finally, the face.

*The* face. The face a billion women wanted to possess, a billion men wanted to find in the mirror every morning. Eyes so blue they made you forget the words *Paul Newman*. Cheeks chiseled with the mastery of a Michelangelo. A chin so perfect photographers wept to capture it so the light just caught that faint cleft.

Perfectly groomed, almost jet black hair. Just a little long, a little rakish. Just brushing the edge of his collarless tux shirt, so that the adoring throngs would know he wasn't really as concerned about his appearance as he might have been. As he had a right to be.

And, according to the myriad reports that crossed wires daily across the world, he really wasn't. It wasn't simply that Cameron Ross was the most devastatingly handsome man in the world. It wasn't that he was the most effortlessly elegant, easily capturing the "new Cary Grant" moniker—actually, the "*finally*, a new Cary Grant" moniker. It wasn't even the fact that the Academy Award nomination he was strolling up the red carpet to see about proved that he wasn't just handsome and elegant and intelligent, but, damn it, talented. It was that he didn't even seem to notice any of it.

"Oh, no," one of the women in the crowd moaned as Cameron reached behind him to take hold of a very feminine, very beautiful hand. "He brought her."

*Her*. Isabelle Renoult, a whisper away from an Academy Award herself, a plea on the lips of almost as many men as women who chanted the name Cameron Ross. Cameron's leading lady for the film for which they'd both captured their nominations, and, unfortunately, his off-again on-again paramour for most of the last two years. Tragically, more on than off. Rumor had it that he was carrying a big ring to go with her Oscar.

She took even longer to emerge from the car, a regal butterfly set free from its sleek cocoon, and all the while Cameron watched her with delighted eyes. And the crowd watched them both, alternately fascinated, enchanted and despairing.

"How does it feel?" the luckiest interviewer breathlessly demanded, shoving the first of a thousand mikes in Cameron's face. "Your first nomination? Do you think the Golden Globe you won will mean a shoo-in for you?"

It seemed that Cameron was oblivious to the jostling, the sweating, the deafening roar of approval from the crowd, the desperation of the various camera people to capture that perfect smile perfectly.

He smiled as if he meant it, and four women in the front row of the peanut gallery fainted dead away.

A man only thirty-three years old should not look so mature. So mysterious. So gently amused, as if he were in on the joke along with everyone else about how undeserving he was of their attention.

"Well," he drawled in that voice that carried just a hint of Oxford in it, "I imagine I could almost get away with saying that I'm not affected by any of this, if Isabelle hadn't been there to catch me all ready in my tux at six o'clock this morning."

Isabelle, a vision in Grace Kelly cheekbones and upswept honey blond hair, smiled. The crowd gushed, and the couple moved on, chatting, smiling, waving, lingering just a little so the people on the street knew they were the ones this enchanted couple would really rather spend time with. They were the people Cameron Ross enjoyed, even though every one of them knew there wasn't a thing they'd have in common with a man who mingled with historians, mathematicians, moguls and princes. A man who played Chopin with the tenderness of a lover and polo with the passion of a predator.

He *was* the new Cary Grant. The man who had single-handedly brought elegance back to film, who kept his private life private and his public life a delight. Who courted brilliant women of legendary beauty and impressed experts on his range of knowledge.

He was charmed, charming, roguish. A raconteur and friend. He was magic; and in that moment, suspended on a brisk, bright California afternoon, the crowds in the streets felt privileged that they had had the chance to even see him.

# One

———

"**H**e's a mess."

He couldn't have agreed more. His head was splitting, his throat was raw, and his mouth tasted as if somebody had served him scrambled socks. Even his stomach, usually immune to his greater follies, was threatening revolt. He was facedown in a bed that smelled like flowers and sunshine, and he thought he'd rather be dead.

"Get on in and finish your breakfast, Hannah," he heard another voice say. "I'll take care of him."

Noah cracked open an eye to find the pair of them standing at the edge of the bed. The smaller of the two—but not by much—was examining him with the considered eye of a skeptic. Freckle-faced, round-cheeked, saucy-eyed and possessing the thickest cap of bright red hair he'd ever seen, he figured her for all of six. She was standing there with her hands on her hips looking like a mother considering a misbehaving boy.

"Dirtier'n a junkyard dog, Mom," she pronounced. "It's a disgrace."

Noah wondered who the heck she was. He didn't remember hearing anything about a child. But then, in the condition he was in, he didn't remember how he got here. He kind of felt like Judy Garland coming to after the trip to Oz. Only everything wasn't in black and white. It was in blinding Technicolor, provided by what he was sure was a five-hundred-watt overhead light.

"Thanks, Hannah," the taller one was saying, her consideration on him, too. "I'll pass that along. Now, scoot."

She gave the little girl a swat to the rump, and Hannah headed out.

Noah winced. Hannah was wearing boots. Noah knew. She set them down just a bit too deliberately against that hardwood floor for it to be unintentional. Her steps clattered like hammer blows around in his head.

The second one was still there, her posture a mirror of the littler one's. Hands on hips, head tilted just a little, eyes wary and bright. The same red hair, although softened, deepened into an auburn that begged for the sun to find it. Same freckles over an oval face. Strong chin and soft mouth. Interesting contrast. Interesting face.

This one he knew, because of the voice. This one he'd asked for. He closed his eye again and just listened to her.

"Mr. Campbell," she said, a little more loudly than the last time. "It's your alarm clock calling."

"Nice to hear it," he managed, his well-trained voice reduced to rubble by the boilermakers the night before, not to mention the myriad variations he'd been consuming the nights before that. "Ms. McCann."

"Then you remember me."

"I hope so. I argued with my partner enough about you."

"You need to get up," she informed him, her tone gaining a layer of authority.

"Can you talk a little more quietly?" he asked, burrowing deeper into the real feather pillow he hadn't noticed before.

"You ignore me when I talk more quietly," she told him. "And I don't have time to be ignored."

"Then I really am here?"

He still didn't open his eyes. He thought he'd just lie here a month or so and enjoy the smell of clean air and coffee, the crisp fold of sheets beneath his grimy cheek. The sensation of that sharp, slim woman standing just out of reach.

"Depends on where you think here is," she said.

"The ranch."

"In that case, you really are here."

He gave his head a minimal nod that ended in a massive scowl. "Oh."

"Bad idea?"

"Only one of many."

"I can well imagine. Do you remember last night?"

Last night. Yes, he remembered last night. He remembered getting into the airport at Bozeman and driving. He remembered thinking that if he just got to the ranch he'd feel better. He'd find what he'd been looking for, for so long, and the grinding disappointment would ease, just a little. The sense of isolation would dissipate.

He remembered finding Westridge at sunset with the sun gilding the snow in the Absaroka Mountains to the east and the wind whistling across the meadows. He remembered the lights of the Last Chance Saloon beckoning him in the gloom. He remembered that nobody knew him there, and that for the first time in a century he'd felt himself relaxing.

Past that...

"Last night?" he echoed gently, gathering up the nerve to inch his hand toward the stubble on his jaw for a good scratch or two. "Oh, yeah. I remember it. At least the first five hours or so. The bartender's name was Rick, and he thought boilermakers were as good an idea as I did."

"You got my ranch hands drunk."

He wanted to laugh. He might have if he hadn't thought it would split his head apart. So he opened an eye and hazarded a look. "I did not hold their mouths open and make them drink."

"You bought them rounds," she countered in that no-nonsense way that had won him over before he'd ever set eyes on her. "Same thing. And we have to brand a couple hundred cattle today. They don't need to be playing with cattle with a thick head."

A sigh. "A point I'll certainly consider much more carefully in the future."

She gave him a bouncing nod. "You made a lot of mostly incoherent noise last night about going out with us this morning. You still interested?"

"Morning? It's morning?"

"It's damn near six minutes to sunrise, son."

He recognized that tone of voice, too. "Do you realize you work for me?" he couldn't help but ask.

She proffered a bright grin that showed off even white teeth and a surprisingly cute dimple in her left cheek. "You find someone else to make this ranch profitable without selling it to a Japanese conglomerate, you can fire me. Now, get up or forget it."

"Then this means I don't get the tour you promised?"

"I promised it when you said you'd be here last week. If you're still upright at the end of the day, I'll give you the abbreviated version. Now, let's go."

He closed his eye again. "I don't suppose we could rethink this tomorrow."

He could hear the scrape of a boot as she swung around for the door. "Fifteen minutes," she threatened. "After that, we're out of here."

Just before she hit the door, she stopped. "By the way, Mr. Campbell. Do you ride?"

That did get a kind of laugh out of him, even though he had his palm pressed to his forehead to ease the pressure. "Yes, Ms. McCann," he assured her. "I ride."

Even if it killed him this morning, he'd ride. He hadn't bought this ranch to sit on the porch and watch somebody else work it. He needed this place, this anchor. He needed this pragmatic woman with her bright green eyes and flashing red hair strangled into its braid to run it for him while he was away, so it would always be there. So something would always be there for him.

"By the way, yourself, Ms. McCann," he said before she could get a good head start on him. "You never mentioned a Hannah in your employment interview."

He thought he'd at least give her pause. He should have known better, even though he'd only met her over the phone. "You never asked, Mr. Campbell."

And then, closing the door without a sound, she was gone.

Dulcy McCann, that was her name. Dulcy. Noah had envisioned a blond girl, all fresh skin and sweet eyes and gingham. Something from a Rogers and Hammerstein musical, that would go with the name.

Dulcy McCann's face went with her voice instead. Pink-cheeked from the wind, sharp edged and wide-eyed, with the kind of mouth that could deliver much harsher judgments in its configuration than its product. A full mouth, with lips that should relax more, so people might know she wasn't quite as hard. Quite as rigid.

She was sleek looking from necessity and hard work rather than fashion. Much too petite to really be able to handle the work, no matter what she said. No matter what the profit-and-loss statements said. A mere slip of a girl, his mother would have said, even in jeans and flannel shirts and down vests. Crackling with energy, possessing a smile like the flash of the sun through a gray sky.

It had been Ethan who'd insisted on letting her stay on as manager when they'd bought the ranch. Ethan who'd done most of the interviews when they'd finally decided to buy the Lazy V. Noah had been too busy in fantasyland to spend the time needed to talk stock and breeding and long-term goals. Noah had been making the obscene money that had allowed him and his cousin to buy a cattle ranch for him to escape to.

And now he was here. He was in the place he'd dreamed about since he'd been six years old and sitting out on the fire escape by Ethan's bedroom. Home. A big white Victorian house with a wrap-around porch where he could sit with coffee after dinner to watch the evening creep across the high mountains. Wide corrals stocked with sturdy quarter horses and meadows dotted in white-faced Herefords, and a nearby river begging to be fished.

He'd been waiting for so long, and they'd gone to such great lengths to get him here. And now he was too hung over to enjoy it. Hell, he was too hung over to even go out there and give his best on the trail.

It didn't mean he wouldn't.

Groaning at the cacophony the movement set up in his head, Noah swung his long legs over the side of the bed and teetered to his feet. He needed to change. He needed to shower. He hadn't cared about doing it for close to two weeks.

Why couldn't Isabelle have seen how good this could be? Why couldn't she have understood?

It didn't matter.

Noah scrubbed his hands through his hair and searched around for the luggage he should have brought with him. He caught sight of a mirror instead.

He couldn't help but offer it a grin. What would his press agent say at that sight? he wondered. His agent would faint dead away. There wasn't a person on earth who would mistake that red-eyed, gray-faced, haggard looking bastard in the mirror for Cameron Ross. Which was just what Noah wanted.

No one in this valley knew who had really bought the Lazy V, and that was the way it was going to stay. Noah had long since perfected the transition from everyman to star, that infinitesimal something that lit the cameras and disappeared in the glare of normal day, the magic that still kept him almost invisible when he wanted to be.

It helped, of course, that the real Noah was nothing like the swashbuckling, sophisticated Cameron people expected. It also helped that Noah had developed a deviously simple diversion to send the press in the wrong direction. He just prayed like hell the people of Montana would see just what they expected and no more. Because what they saw was the truth.

Cameron Ross lived in Hollywood where fantasy was the coin of the realm. The man who came to the ranch was Noah Campbell.

She didn't even knock on the door. Just swung it open as if unconcerned with what she'd find inside. There was just a little too much humor in those sharp green eyes for Noah to think she didn't know exactly what she was doing, though.

"Here," she said, tossing a pile of clothing at him. "The sheriff didn't bring your luggage along with you last night. Since you were already wearing your boots, you can use some of Slim's work stuff until you get the rest."

Noah all but blanched. "The sheriff?"

Dulcy McCann tilted her head again. "Oh, yeah. I hope you wanted to make a grand entrance, Mr. Campbell. Cause you sure did."

And then, before he could talk back to her, she walked on out.

I have an Oscar, Noah thought in consternation as he stared at the closed door. I own a house in Malibu, a townhouse in New York and the entire damn island of St. Denis. I have women across the world sending me their underwear in the mail. Why should I put up with this?

Because this was the smoothest running ranch in Montana, and Dulcy McCann didn't have a clue who he was. That was why.

Suddenly beset by the urge to whistle, Noah Campbell tossed his borrowed clothing over his shoulder and headed into the bathroom for a quick shower.

Dulcy reached the kitchen at warp speed hoping nobody would notice that the color in her cheeks wasn't just windburn. What a way to start out a morning. What a way to start a week of branding. She had a thousand things to do, a million things to keep in her mind. And from the moment she'd walked into that bedroom this morning, all she'd been able to think about was the man who was now her boss.

Brother. Just what she needed.

She needed this job, this ranch. She needed the chance to do what she did best. And she needed to do it with a free enough hand that the whispers of surprise and outrage would settle a little around Westridge at the idea that little Dulcy McCann was manager of a spread like the Lazy V.

She did not need to keep fighting the absurd impulse to grin.

Dulcy wasn't sure what she'd thought had lurked behind that honeyed baritone voice she'd deliberately courted over the phone for six weeks last fall while they'd been finalizing the various deals.

A businessman. A man accustomed to wielding power and money. She could have figured that out from the balance sheets, the influx of capital for breeding stock and renovations on the property, the terse, knowledgeable questions and answers. A man who made a dollar stretch to its limit, but a solid, sensible man who hadn't let the little idea of a woman running his place get in the way of recognizing that woman's ability.

She hadn't expected the man she'd just faced, though. She hadn't expected him to open his eyes and damn near knock her off her feet.

Blue. His eyes were blue. Blue the color of a late-afternoon mountain sky. Blue the color of the morning glories that wrapped around the arbor in the back. Blue...

"Mom? Is he goin'?"

Startled, Dulcy looked up to find Hannah standing in front of her, holding out a cup of coffee. Dulcy considered the sharp consideration of her daughter as she accepted the offering.

She still wanted to smile. She wanted to rub at her chest where the perfectly unreasonable bubble of attraction had suddenly lodged.

"Thanks, puddin'. Yeah, he's goin'. You ready for Aunt Sally to take you to music camp?"

Hannah pulled a face. "Mom, that bus doesn't leave for two more hours."

Dulcy hid her consternation behind her first sip of coffee. "I knew that. I was just testing you. You helping Aunt Sally?"

"No. I'm helpin' you. Do you like him, Mom? Is he okay?"

*Is he going to let us stay?* Dulcy could hear the unasked question as clearly as if Hannah had given in and asked it. Hannah, her baby, was the most outrageously gifted kid in five states. She could do, and would do, anything. *If* she had her feet planted firmly under her. If she knew just what to expect from life. And poor little Hannah hadn't been able to know what to expect for a long time.

"We have a contract," Dulcy assured the little girl, a hand to her cheek. "It doesn't matter whether we have warts or play the piano at midnight while he's here. If we make the ranch work, we stay."

That won a harrumph that sounded suspiciously like the ones Hank Bellows dispatched down around the corrals. "I don't believe *we* were the ones making noise at midnight."

Dulcy grinned. "More like two. I think he'll be okay. The sheriff said something about some lady jilting him."

Hannah's great brown eyes grew to astonishing proportions. "Jilted him? *Him?* Is she crazy? He's gorgeous!"

Then Dulcy hadn't been hallucinating. She frowned, anyway. "I thought you said he looked like a junkyard dog."

"A gorgeous junkyard dog. Becky and Amy are gonna be jealous when they find out we have a guy in our house who looks like him."

That stopped Dulcy in mid-sip. Oh, boy. That wasn't what she needed, either. Another rumor. Another reason to suggest that Dulcy had gotten her job for the wrong reasons, kept it for the wrong reasons.

"Uh, Hannah, do me a favor. Wait on that a week or so. Can you do that?"

Hannah rolled her eyes, which, on a munchkin in a starched cotton shirt and perfectly pressed jeans, looked suspiciously adult. "I may explode or something."

"Think of it this way. When they find out what he looks like, you can look surprised and say, 'Oh, you think so? Well, he's almost as good-lookin' as my dad was.' That'll really get their goat."

The idea seemed to work. "Was he really?"

"He was."

Really.

"Get over here and eat something before you leave," a new participant chimed in. "It's gonna be a long day."

A hand out to tousle her daughter's hair, Dulcy looked up to acknowledge her cook, housekeeper, everywoman and favorite cousin. Sally stood in the middle of the big red-and-white kitchen with a towel draped over her ample shoulder and flour speckled liberally over even more generous breasts.

Sally was from the German branch of the family and carried the resemblance like a family seal. Blond hair, blue eyes, apple cheeks and ample girth. She smiled always and imparted hugs as healing as tonics. Sally was four years older than Dulcy and was graced with a natural affinity for home and hearth. Dulcy thanked providence that it was Dulcy's home and hearth she usually graced.

"Pancakes?" Dulcy almost begged.

Sally's smile was like a mother's. "Banana. With a little of Homer Thompson's sage sausage."

Hannah headed for her coat and the back door, and Dulcy walked into the kitchen to partake of Sally's gastronomical delights and pragmatic support.

The kitchen, as ever, when Sally was working, was a mess. Pots, pans, griddles everywhere, all awash in food fixings. Sally considered food a high art and practiced it like a magician. It was just that her rabbits tended to fall on the floor with disconcerting regularity.

"He really is a looker, huh?" she asked.

Out of sight of Hannah, who was already out the door to say goodbye to the horses and ranch hands, Dulcy rolled her own eyes. "I was expecting Ted Turner. I got Gary Cooper instead."

Sally's smile was salacious. "Makes comin' to work worthwhile. He married?"

"Freshly jilted. That's what all the noise was about last night. He and the boys were evidently seeing the lady off to fairer pastures, at least in spirit. Spirits."

"I like a man who mourns a woman," Sally decided, reaching up to one of the maple cabinets to pull out a huge bottle of aspirin. Then she produced a bottle of Bloody Mary mix with which to chase it down. "It's kinda like Indiana Jones, when he lost Marian. My favorite scene in the movie."

Sally punctuated all her conversations with movie references. Everything reminded her of a movie or something she'd read about somebody who'd made a movie. Or a TV show. Or commercials about TV shows.

"The Nazis didn't get Mr. Campbell's girlfriend, Sally," Dulcy advised her dryly as she finished off the dregs of her coffee. "She walked out."

Sally was nodding as she cracked two raw eggs into the Bloody Mary mix. "Just like *Affair to Remember*."

"*She* was hit by a car."

Sally also usually got the reference wrong.

"It didn't make Cary Grant any happier." Sally often did eventually get around to something resembling a valid point. "Is he eating breakfast?"

Dulcy scooped up her own pancakes while Sally mixed the boss's tonic. "Cary Grant?" Dulcy retorted. "I doubt it."

"The junkyard dog."

"I'm not going to last through too many more junkyard dog references," a throaty voice announced from the doorway.

Both women looked up to find their new boss slouching against the door frame as if unsure whether the floor was going to behave and stay in its place.

Sally, never at a loss for words, simply handed him the thick red concoction. "Here," she offered. "Hangover juice."

Noah Campbell actually smiled. "God bless you."

"I'm Sally." She introduced herself as she wiped flour-dusted hands across her white apron and faded jeans. "Cook, housekeeper and busybody."

Noah Campbell took her hand as if they were at a cocktail party. "Noah Campbell. A pleasure to meet you."

Dulcy knew she should have said something. Anything. She couldn't quite manage it. For some reason he startled her. Unsettled her. It wasn't just the fact that he was a lot taller than she'd thought. But then again, the night before he'd been inspecting his shoe tops as she and Bart Bixby had dragged him back to the guest room.

It wasn't the way his just-wet hair curled past his collar where a woman would find her fingers itching to be at it, a length and lazy cut no self-respecting businessman would allow. It wasn't the soft Texan drawl that seemed to make his words into living things that curled around a woman's soft places and make her smile.

It wasn't the fact that he had evidently decided not to shave, which gave the gulleys on his face deeper shadow and blurred the edges of his jaw. Dulcy couldn't imagine a hotshot business mogul allowing himself to do that, either, but then, shaving was one of the great personal choices in Montana. If you wanted to grow a beard, you might as well do it here. And Dulcy had the feeling that Noah Campbell had the makings of a slam-bang beard.

It wasn't even that he looked dangerous, although he did. It wasn't that, even disheveled and wearing somebody else's clothes, he generated an aura of power that made Dulcy feel suddenly foolish and incompetent, which he also did.

It wasn't that he seemed sharper or less sharp. No, it was...

His eyes. He looked up at her, and Dulcy forgot her pancakes. Had she been hallucinating before? She could have sworn she'd seen blue eyes. Blue, blue eyes. They were gray now. Quiet, reasonable, perfectly respectable gray eyes, and suddenly that face that had taken her breath, merely made her pause.

Well, almost.

"You wearing contacts?" was all she could think of to say, even as she wiped her own palm down the sides of her jeans.

Even Sally stared at her. Dulcy was sure it was because the last thing a sane person should notice on this man was contact lenses.

He straightened a little as he took a huge slug of juice and grimaced with the best of them. "Is there a ban around here on nearsighted people riding horses? I thought that was only pilots."

Dulcy could feel the heat flooding right back into her cheeks. "Pancakes?" she offered instead. "Sally makes the best in the country."

He looked over to the well-used oak table, where Dulcy had already set out her stack of pancakes alongside Sally's latest batch of reading material, and lost whatever color he had. "Uh, no thanks. Not now. I think I'd like to get outside."

"You're going to have to eat soon," Sally told him. "Long day out there."

He nodded, finished off his breakfast in a gulp and set the glass on the white countertop before heading for the door. "Thanks, anyway. Which way's the barn?"

He was already halfway across the red tile floor on his way to the back door before Dulcy had the presence of mind to answer.

"Just keep going in a straight line. When you get there, introduce yourself. You already met Hannah. She'll introduce you to Hank, and he'll introduce you to your horse."

"And you?"

"*Do* want my breakfast. I'll be down in a minute. And see if anybody has an extra hat to fit you."

He didn't even turn around. "I have a hat."

Yeah, she thought. Something straight out of an L.L. Bean catalogue to go with those brand-new, unscuffed boots you're wearing. Something that hadn't had a chance to build up a good sweat ring around the crown. Something that still needed to be crushed and swatted and beaten down until it was soft and familiar, the kind of hat that made you want to grab at it . . .

"You have a hat in Westridge," she said abruptly. "You need one here, today."

He just nodded and headed out the door.

For a second, left behind, the women simply stared after him as his shadow drifted off through the predawn gray.

"*DOA,*" Sally said.

Dulcy translated that to mean, he looks as good as Dennis Quaid did in *DOA*, all nasty and sad.

"*Lost Weekend,*" Dulcy retorted evenly and headed over to where her pancakes were getting cold.

Sally watched her. "This is going to be harder than you thought."

Dulcy plopped down in a chair and purposefully picked up knife and fork. "No it isn't. He'll come play cowboy for six weeks and then go home to Philadelphia where he belongs."

Uh-huh. And in the morning the ranch would be all hers and there would be peace on earth.

As she reached for the syrup, Dulcy noticed that Sally had already bought her week's supply of celebrity gossip. It was piled to the left of the butter like gaudy picture slides. "So," she said, turning her attention back to her meal. "What's-his-name is going to marry Isabelle Renoult, huh?"

If anything would get Sally's attention away from the subject matter at hand, it was the lovelife of one of her favorite stars. Sally knew more about the horoscope-related prospects of every inhabitant of Los Angeles, Aspen and Santa Fe, than she did about a thousand things to do with flour. Just by this tabloid alone, Sally would have learned that Cameron Ross was engaged, Kevin Costner was expecting twins with a belly dancer, and Lisa Marie Presley was in contact with her father through a Sudanese channeler named Rao.

Dulcy thought she'd scored a hit when Sally sat herself down in another chair, her usual "dispensing of insider information" position.

"You don't care who Cameron Ross is going to marry," she accused. "You care about what Noah Campbell can do to you. When does he find out what's going on, Dulce?"

Dulcy shot her cousin a cautionary glare. "If I can help it, he won't."

"Dulcy..."

Dulcy suddenly lost her taste for pancakes. Shoving her chair back, she got up and headed for her own hat. "If he finds out, we won't have a ranch to run anymore, Sally. And I refuse to consider that option."

"He's not a stupid man."

Dulcy slowed to a stop, her sight drawn out beyond the back window to where she could see the shadows of men and horses shifting impatiently down by the corral. It was the busy time of the year. Herds needed to be moved to fresh grazing land, stock evaluated and some sold, gardens and feed crops tended to. And this week, calves on five different ranches in the valley had to be branded, dehorned, castrated and vaccinated. Dulcy had all she could handle just to get it all done with the handful of men she employed. On top of that, she had the boss in for a visit. The hung-over boss. The handsome, magnetic hung-over boss. The hung-over smart boss who might just expose the truth and take away her chance to retrieve her name.

She couldn't let that happen.

She wouldn't.

No matter what happened.

Without another word to Sally, Dulcy opened the back door and walked out into the dawn light, ready to lie through her teeth.

# Two

———

**M**anure. Noah sucked in the distinctive tang of it and thought how very far from Los Angeles he was. How he preferred the sharp, distinctive aroma of well-fed horses to the musk of exhaust and power. Horses and hay, leather and liniment, man sweat and more coffee. Dawn air and dirt.

Not a person on the planet would believe that Cameron Ross would find himself brought to a halt in the middle of a predawn pasture, sniffing the air like a sommelier testing an old Château Margeaux. He didn't care. The ground was hard and uneven beneath his boots, the men taciturn at his approach. The horses danced and whuffled a bit with impatience as they waited to be loaded onto the horse trailer that waited by the barn. Mist curled from the ground like thin smoke, and birds were beginning to wake in the trees. The morning was perfect.

Noah's head was threatening to split open like a rotten cantaloupe. His stomach was heaving from whatever that woman had introduced to it, and he was still trying to get over the sight of himself grinning out from the cover of that rag on the kitchen table. It didn't matter. He was beginning to feel better.

He hadn't been recognized. Not even a quizzical glance. There were not cameras in the bushes, no sleazy innuendo about his need to mount a horse or hide in the mountains. As far as the world knew, he wasn't here.

But he was.

He was home.

"Mr. Campbell," the little girl was saying in that no-nonsense tone of voice of hers. "Do you want to meet Hank or not?"

Well, Noah had to give the women in this outfit credit. They didn't worry any about insulting the boss.

"Yes," he told her, lifting the too-big hat from his head and taking a swipe at his hair.

One of the men stepped forward, a huge, slow-moving, steely eyed specimen Noah couldn't remember seeing at the bar the night before.

"You got my men drunk," Hank immediately said, squinting down his broad nose at Noah, who came up to his chin.

Noah felt like sighing. Didn't anybody read the employment agreement around here?

But then, the attitude here was refreshing after the warm bath of obeisance he'd been paddling around in, in L.A.

"I bought rounds," he said evenly. "I didn't know the men accepting them worked here. Not till it was too late."

He actually got a round of tender chuckles for that one. It had been a grand evening. At least until one of the men, a Hispanic kid named Paco, had admitted that they all had to be up and saddled in fewer than four hours.

Hank squinted even harder, as if he had a hard time figuring this Eastern greenhorn out. "You ride?"

Noah nodded. "I ride."

"Ever rode a cow pony?"

"Matter of fact, I have. It's been a while, though."

Hank nodded, his eyes still tight with withheld opinions.

"I think he can handle him, boss," one of the men piped up. "Give him a shot."

Hank swung a steely glare at the hapless man. "Hannah's gone for him."

Noah hadn't realized that Hannah had separated herself from the inquisition until she returned, leading a solid buckskin gelding.

"His name is Doofus," she said with a straight face.

Noah considered the animal. "You're kidding."

"Don't make fun of him," Hannah warned, with just a trace of childish concern in that prim voice. "He's sensitive."

"I'll bet."

Noah was a fairly good judge of horses, and this one was a good one. A solid quarter horse with the high tail and arched neck of an Arabian and the delicate head of a mustang. He had intelligent eyes, and ears that were on a constant swivel to catch all the action. Nosy bugger. Noah liked that in a horse.

He solemnly accepted the reins from Hannah and began to get acquainted. The minute he took control, the horse danced away, his ears flattening. Noah smiled, crooned a little and rubbed at the horse's withers until he settled.

"We're goin' to the Wheelright," Hank said. "First ranch on the dance card. You want, you can help corral the herd so we can get 'em down and done."

Noah knew better than to ask what they needed doing that needed them to be down for. He assumed branding. "Is Ms. McCann coming along?"

That provoked another round of chuckles. "Oh, yeah," one of the hands spoke up. "The Big D's comin'. She wouldn't miss a chance to show us what she'd like to do to us all."

Hank's attention swiveled again, completely silencing the man. Noah didn't react to the interplay. He stored it away for later retrieval. There had been a lot of bitterness in that voice. A truckload of frustration.

And no argument from the other men, either when the first man spoke or when Hank silenced him.

"All right," Hank said, turning for the trailer. "Let's go."

And that was that. Six men exploded into action, and horses all over the yard were turned toward the trailer. Noah noticed again that it was Hannah who led Doofus. And Doofus who responded quietly, easily and with just a few playful nips to Hannah's hair, which made her look up and grin.

"Doofus isn't your horse, is he?" Noah asked, walking alongside.

Hannah looked almost abashed. "Oh, no, sir. My horse is a pony. Esmerelda. Doofus and I are just friends."

Noah nodded. "I'll take good care of him."

"You wanna ride with the bo—" Hank stopped short and scratched at his cheek. "Uh, wanna ride with Dulcy? Gonna be crowded in the truck."

"Don't mind callin' her the boss," Noah assured the man. "She is. For now, at least, I can only get here to visit."

Hank's expression betrayed the fact that he hadn't decided how he wanted to take that particular arrangement yet. Noah was about to say something else when he forgot what it was. For some reason he found himself turning toward the big white house up the hill.

Dulcy.

Funny, he hadn't even heard the door slam. Couldn't really hear her tread across the grass. Even so, he'd realized she'd been closing in as certainly as he knew where every camera was when he was working a film. It was a sixth sense he'd never extended to women before.

Interesting.

Noah had the most unsettled feeling that *interesting* wasn't really the word he wanted.

"Ready to go, Dulcy," Hank said, alongside.

Noah knew he should be listening to Hank's tone of voice. Was he deferential? Patronizing? Long-suffering? It would say a lot about how the ranch was run.

The minute Noah caught sight of his manager, though, he couldn't seem to think past incongruities. Mixed messages. Her hair was shoved up beneath a battered beige Stetson, and her stride was brisk. It didn't manage to mask the sensuality of her gait, though, her slim hips swinging just a little as she walked, her face a too-soft bloom hidden beneath that hat like a mayflower beneath its umbrella of leaves.

Noah had come to concentrate on horses and cattle and open air. He was having a hell of a time doing that, all of a sudden.

"How 'bout you, Mr. Campbell?" she asked, just a crust of contest in her pleasant, throaty voice. "You ready to go?"

She was pulling on leather gloves and held another, larger pair, which she handed over to Noah.

"If Doofus is ready, so am I," he said with a smile.

Her eyes, he thought inconsequentially as he took the gloves from her. He wanted to see her eyes better beneath that shadow. Her eyes were almost translucent, gray and soft as mist.

For just a second, Noah thought she might have been having a little problem looking away, too.

"Who's staying?" she asked Hank, her turn toward her foreman abrupt.

This time Noah couldn't mistake the fractional raising of the eyebrow that betrayed the old man's surprise. "Billy Boy. You know how he is."

She nodded. "Make sure he takes care of the irrigation while we're gone."

"Done."

Nobody thought it necessary to explain or clear their decisions with the man who controlled their livelihoods, Noah realized, and felt the pressures of the other world lift a notch farther away. He was all but invisible here. It was all that he wanted.

Or it had been until he'd opened his eyes to see just what kind of manager he'd hired.

He was suffering from Isabelle's rejection. Her insistence in loving the man he only pretended to be. He was a prime candidate for a bad rebound.

None of that seemed to be making a bit of difference to the part of his anatomy that responded to soft gray eyes and lithe figures.

"All right, Mr. Campbell," Dulcy was saying, her eyes hidden beneath the brim of that big hat, as she wrestled keys from her pocket and headed for the battered pickup in the yard. "Let's go rope us some cattle."

Not the kind of invitation a man got from a pretty woman every day. Just the kind Noah wanted on a morning like this. Pulling on his own gloves, he headed over to the passenger door and climbed in.

Noah wasn't sure what he'd expected. The only cow time he'd done had been on his uncle's small ranch in Texas. He'd never done a big spread before. He'd certainly never joined a pool of ranchers and cowboys who worked their way up a valley getting the branding done for every ranch in sight within a week.

The ranchers all worked together, Dulcy had explained as she'd deftly steered the truck over some of the most difficult back roads in the country. If they didn't, they wouldn't have the manpower at the all-important branding season. Everybody pooled hands and got the job done quickly, efficiently and almost painlessly.

She'd warned him, as they'd led the horse trailer down over a low pass and into the main scoop of the valley beyond, that there would be dust and noise and blood and the worst language this side of a baseball dugout. She'd warned him that he would work hard and hurt worse by the end of the day. She'd warned him that they wouldn't take time for him to get up to speed, so he should just follow Paco and do whatever he did.

She hadn't warned him that every rancher who showed up would seem more interested in grilling him than charring cattle.

"Philadelphia?" Walt Stewart from the Flying Diamond demanded, hands shoved in his threadbare jeans pockets, his legs bowed, his teeth stained with tobacco juice, his eyes flinty and sharp. "Whatcha doin' here?"

Other eyes watched him answer. Other arms remained crossed in silent mistrust well into the day, no matter how cordial and helpful the men were.

"I spent a lot of time as a kid working my uncle's ranch in Texas."

"Why didn't you buy there?"

"Too flat. Too dry."

Everybody waited for some other answer. "Philadelphia," Walt repeated, as if testing the sound of it. "Just don't make sense."

"You don't live somewhere else now?" another of the owners asked as he sipped at his coffee.

"Like where?"

"California," Mike Murphy said much too quickly.

Ah. Yes. Now Noah understood. When Noah had started looking for his ranch, he'd tried the area around Bozeman. Unfortunately, Bozeman already wasn't Bozeman anymore. The Hollywood community, embracing the wide outdoors the way they had EST and yoga, had descended on the sleepy Western city and turned it into a kind of mongrel Aspen. In valleys all along the continental divide, obscenely wealthy people had grabbed good land and tucked it away so no one could use it. They had brought in herds of elk and buffalo and had forbidden generations-old access to hunting and fishing areas and high grazing pastures. They'd tarted up the towns and skyrocketed the taxes. Noah had seen the first Gelato stand in Westridge, and knew that these men had a right to be afraid. Just not of him.

"Philadelphia," he said evenly, slurping down the rest of his own dregs before the quick break ended.

The cattle were in the holding pens. It was now time to drive the young bulls down one chute and the heifers down another. Castrating, branding and ear-tagging were the activities of the day.

"You know," Walt said, not exactly looking at Noah but at the ground he was scuffing with his sharp-toed boot. "There's an access way to the Little Ridge River on your property. Not to mention those high mountains."

Noah hadn't known. He guessed that came with the guided tour he hadn't gotten yet. "Uh-huh."

Six pair of eyes drilled him like lasers. "You gonna close it off?"

"Why would I do that?"

"Privacy."

Noah snorted. "You ever been to Philadelphia, Walt?"

"Can't say as I have."

"Then let me be the first to tell you. I have more privacy in my barn than I have in the entire city of Philadelphia."

"My access to public grazing is through your west pastures," another rancher offered, almost diffidently. Noah heard the warring emotions in the man's voice and felt for him. Furious at having to ask, terrified at the answer. Caught right between everything he'd known and what was coming.

Noah gave him special attention. A thin man, with the gnarled hands of a lifetime's work and the sharp tan line of a man who had always lived in the high sun.

"You're next door, aren't you?" Noah asked.

There was a small dip of the head. A tiny easing of posture as age-old hospitality warred with defenses. "Cletus Wilson."

Noah nodded and extended his hand for a quick shake, as if they'd just met. "My pleasure, Cletus. What does Dulcy say about it?" he asked.

"Dulcy?" Walt Stewart retorted with a broad grin. "What's she got to do with it?"

"She's in charge," Noah assured all the men.

The reactions this time were telling. A quick range from amazement to distrust to acceptance. It was Walt Stewart who spoke up.

"Surely you can't think that little girl's gonna handle all that herself. I mean, she tries an' all . . ."

"Always been a feisty one," another man said.

"That don' mean—"

Noah felt it again. A tickle at the base of his neck. A crowding of dust-thickened air. He didn't see her, but she was close by.

"You're not going to put Hank in charge?" Cletus asked sincerely.

Noah proffered a look of blank innocence. "Why would I do that?"

"Because...well, because...well, we just figured Dulcy was temporary. Till you got here and all."

"Now, Walt," Mike Murphy spoke up easily. "Dulcy's worked hard over there. Can't take that from her, no matter what."

The answering shrugs were small, but Mike Murphy kept smiling. A big, self-assured man with a broad smile and premature snowy white hair over pale eyes. "You can count on us all to help if you need it," he said almost needlessly. "If you're gonna let her stay on."

"Unless I catch her stealing my cattle and selling 'em to Kevin Costner," Noah said. "I can't think of a reason to change things."

That was when he realized where she was. Just on the other side of the barn, hidden from sight. Waiting. Not wanting the men to know she'd eavesdropped.

"Hey, you guys work for the government or something?" she yelled, striding up as if she'd been at full steam from the far corrals. "We got cattle to brand."

For no reason at all Noah smiled. If a person looked, he wouldn't even notice that she'd heard. She was grinning and swaggering like any one of the hands he'd seen that morning, her hands shoved into back pockets and her hat pushed back. More at home on this ground than he or Mike Murphy or even Walt Stewart. She was sharp and strong and exciting, and she was the last thing Noah needed in his life right now.

"Where do you need me, boss?" he asked, dropping the ceramic mug on the picnic table with the others and pulling his gloves back out of his belt.

Dulcy squinted up at him as if sizing him up. "You're doin' just fine where you are with Paco," she admitted, and Noah realized he'd been complimented. "Okay with you?"

He fingered the brim of his hat and grinned. "Yes ma'am."

Her eyes widened a fraction. She knew. She realized that he'd seen her back there. That he'd enjoyed baiting the men, like a game. An answering grin caught the corners of her mouth, striking that dimple into her cheek.

"You got the knife?" Mike asked her.

She nodded. "It's what I do best, huh, Uncle Mike?"

"Sure is, sweetie." Tweaking her nose, the big man turned for the cattle and led all the other men with him.

" 'Uncle Mike'?" Noah asked.

Dulcy faced him, her features gathered into a semblance of nonchalance. "Sure. Didn't I tell you? He's the successful side of the family. You two should really hit it off. He's another entrepreneur, just like you."

"Any other family members I should know about?"

She grinned. "I'm related to half the valley. But don't let that intimidate you."

"The half that wants you to keep your job, or the half that thinks you're . . . feisty?"

That got the grin back, full wattage. Bright and brash enough to make Noah's toes curl in his boots. "*Feisty* isn't the word most of my family calls me," she allowed, then eased that grin toward pure mischief. "Especially when I'm wielding a castrating knife."

Noah flinched, just the way she'd wanted. "Is that a subtle warning?"

Dulcy laughed. "I never give warnings," she assured him, turning on her heel. "I just attack. Now, let's work."

Noah swung back up on Doofus and turned him toward where he saw Paco riding drag. He took his place alongside, letting his horse and the ranch dogs do most of the work, while he ate most of the dust. He listened to the unrelenting chorus of calves bawling, of men yelling, of dogs barking. He felt himself settle into the pattern on a good horse, bumping cattle with his knee as they were edged to the chutes, wiping the sweat off his forehead with a forearm and feeling the high sun hot on the back of his neck.

It was dirty, noisy, sometimes dangerous work, performed like a thundering ballet by the experienced men who had done this their entire lives. Smooth and swift and communicated via ribald jokes and obscene epithets.

And there, in the middle of it, just where he could see her through the dust and crowd of bodies, was Dulcy. Armed with the sharpest knives he'd ever seen. Smaller than any living creature in this yard, sweating and red-faced and focused on the job at hand.

She worked the knife like a surgeon, so fast a man barely had time to flinch before another serving of Rocky Mountain oysters was available and the calf was back up on his feet and stumbling back to Mama. Working around the men who helped as if born to it, bred to it.

Even in sweat-soaked shirt and filthy jeans and battered old hat, she was striking. Lithe and supple and as agile as a prima ballerina.

And not one of the men realized it.

Not one of the men saw past the fact that the job was getting done. Not one of the men, for that time, noticed she was a woman.

Noah shouldn't have, either.

He did.

Oh, he did.

He also realized, sitting here atop a well-trained horse alongside a good working hand, that if he did anything about it, he'd lose the best manager in the valley.

It was going to be a very long six weeks after all.

# Three

———

"**Y**ou sore?" Dulcy asked, stepping out of the shadows.

Noah Campbell turned from where he'd been currying Doofus with slow, almost hypnotic strokes. "I think 'rode hard and put up wet' about covers it."

Dulcy had no idea what she was doing here. She had bills to pay, feed orders to place, hay to begin harvesting. She had a sore back, sorer legs and another day just like today scheduled for tomorrow, which meant she should at least have been in a hot bath. Instead she found herself right back in the barn as if she hadn't already spent her entire day with animals.

He was her boss, she rationalized. In charge, in control of their small lives. It had nothing to do with the fact that she swore she could have sensed him a mile away in a snowstorm, or the fact that she kept wanting to see him smile just one more time.

"The rest of the ranchers were pretty darned impressed today," she admitted, shoving her hands into jeans pockets. Digging her toe into the dirt like a shy teen. "Not to mention the hands here. You know, of course, that they expected Doofus to dump you within ten minutes."

"I figured as much. Guess I'm lucky that I've always seemed to get along with horses."

*Get along* wasn't the expression Dulcy would have used. She'd seen him work the buckskin with hands and knees and heels. Gentle, insistent, never once letting the horse get his head.

Doofus was a good horse. One of the best. But Doof could smell an amateur at fifty paces and leave him in the dust every time. He'd never so much as twitched the whole day.

Dulcy should have told Noah that. She couldn't manage more than a rather lame, "You handled yourself well for a—"

"Greenhorn?" He grinned, and she could feel it without looking up. "I'm hardly that."

He was, though. An outsider. He should have been more uncomfortable with the animals, more tentative looking, seated atop a horse. He'd looked like a myth though, all unconscious grace and power, as if he'd been the one born in this valley instead of her.

"Even so..."

"Even so," Noah admitted, "I'm going to feel like hell in the morning. I promise."

Dulcy looked up in surprise. "You're going out again?"

Why couldn't his eyes have been darker? Why couldn't he have been soft and small, an anonymous banker in razor-pressed jeans and L.L. Bean's best?

His clothes had arrived, though, soft, well-worn cotton shirts and battered boots, and a Stetson that had seen as much action as hers.

And his jeans. The quickest way to spot an outsider was his jeans. Ranchers wore Wrangler jeans, because the seams were on the outside of the leg where they wouldn't chafe when you rode. Outsiders never worried about chafing.

Noah Campbell's seams ran down the outside of his leg, and the knees and backside of his jeans were pale with wear. And they fit so well, not too tight, showing off powerful thighs and a butt that would have made the cowboy hall of fame. Dulcy caught herself looking, imagining...

"Dulcy?"

She blinked...blushed, furious that she'd been caught drifting when she hadn't allowed so much as a stray thought since Hannah had been born. "I'm sorry. I'm a little tired myself. What did you say?"

Noah looked amused, as if he knew exactly what she was thinking. God, she hoped not. If he did, she'd be out of a job fast. He would realize that she had known exactly where he'd been all day, simply by feeling the electricity that seemed to build as he got closer.

"I said," he repeated, putting down the curry comb and patting Doof on the rump, "that I don't consider this ranch a ride at Disneyland. If it's a working ranch, then I work when I'm here."

Dulcy dared a direct glance and found herself almost short of breath. "Well, you'll get your money's worth on this trip, then," she managed to say, wondering how she could sound so unaffected. Her palms were sweating, and he was still ten feet away.

This was not going to be the breeze she'd thought it would be when all she'd had to worry about was impressing the boss with the size and health of his herd.

"I do have one question," Noah said, leading Doofus back into his stall and shutting it.

Dulcy concentrated on the bits of hay at her feet. "Shoot."

"My tour. When am I going to get it?"

She looked up again to find him closer, too close. She could feel that odd shimmer along her skin, as if he gave off static charge. "Tour?"

"Tour."

Tour. Tour. Dulcy nodded abruptly. "Sure. I can show you around the buildings after supper. The rest of the ranch will have to wait till we brand and get the herd up to summer pasture. Okay?"

"And the computer?"

The computer. The core of the operation, where all data was kept and updated every day on the running of the ranch: how many head of cattle, weight, growth, price, cost, lineage.

Numbers.

Where the truth lay. The last place Dulcy wanted the boss playing around, until she had everything straightened out.

She did her best not to react. "How 'bout at the end of the week when I'm not so bone tired."

He nodded, his own hands in his jeans pockets, his own posture just a little stiff. "Did you say supper?"

That quickly, Noah was grinning, a deprecating light in his eyes that made Dulcy want to laugh.

"Oh, supper. Sure. That's why I came to get you."

He made her feel like an idiot. Dulcy did not like feeling like an idiot. She wanted to hate him for it, to run his ranch in spite of him.

She had the most horrible feeling it wasn't going to turn out like that at all.

"Well, let's go," he urged, waving her ahead of him. "Besides being sore, I'm so hungry I was beginning to size Doofus up for the grill."

Dulcy found herself chuckling as she preceded him out into the dusk. "Oh, Lord, don't do that. Hannah would never forgive either of us."

"She really likes him, huh?"

"*Like* never came into it. When he was a colt I used to catch her out in his stall sleeping next to him."

"Not anymore?"

She grinned. "That's baby stuff, now. Now she has—"

As if on cue, there issued from the house a blat of noise that made both of them cringe to a halt.

Noah looked up as if expecting the noise to be followed by an explosion.

"What was that?" he demanded.

Dulcy spent a fraction of a second thinking that she could distract him by pointing out the magnificent colors of the sunset, the hawk that was circling in silhouette, the soft mist seeping over the hills to diffuse the remaining light.

Then the noise happened again, and she knew she had no choice.

"Hannah," she said.

Noah stared at her. "You're going to tell me she has a pet elephant tucked up there somewhere?"

"Worse," she admitted. "A trumpet."

That seemed to bring him to a full stop, just at the edge of the yard. Overhead the cottonwood was whispering in the last breeze, and birds chattered in annoyance.

"A trumpet," he said with a scowl.

Dulcy almost closed her eyes. "She's very passionate about it."

*Bl-a-a-a-t—blaaat.*

"Uh-huh."

Dulcy sighed. "I'll have her practice somewhere else."

"Like where, Utah?"

Against her better judgment, Dulcy grinned. Hannah would never understand their gentle mocking. She'd never survive if she heard about it. But Dulcy couldn't help it.

"No. Utah threw us out."

*Blaaat-blaaat-bla-a-a-a-t.*

"I bet." Still neither of them moved, even though the mouth-watering smell of dinner was drifting down the hill like the mist. "Isn't she a little young for something that . . . loud?"

"Yes, she is. But she's already mastered the violin, and she's taken the piano as far as she can go until she gets a little better fingerspan on her. She's been playing since she was four."

"I thought she was four now."

"Six. Almost seven."

"Ah."

"Hannah needs challenges. Music seems to come so easily to her that she has to keep escalating things to keep committed."

"Oh, God," he groaned. "That means that by the time I leave again, she will have worked her way up to tuba."

"I keep praying she discovers the harp. I've heard that'd keep her busy for years."

He sighed. "The trumpet."

"I'll have her stop."

"No. Don't be silly. This is her home. I'll just . . . I'll . . . uh, figure out when she practices and make sure I'm out exercising one of the horses or something."

Dulcy nodded, relaxing just a little. "Good idea. And thank you."

"Mo-o-o-om," Hannah yelled from the front porch. "Aunt Sally says the meat's gettin' cold, the Jell-O's getting hot, and she wants to go home!"

"Coming, honey!"

They resumed their journey, more companionable than they'd been in the barn.

"I thought Sally lived here, too," Noah said.

"No. She lives with her husband. That'd be Bart Bixby, my cousin from the other side of the family. He's sheriff."

"Of course he is. I thought nepotism went out of style."

"Maybe in Philadelphia. Not here."

"Hey, Dulcy."

Dulcy startled like a kid caught with her hand in the drawer. She hadn't even heard Josh approach. She hadn't heard anything but the soft drawl of Noah's voice, and that wouldn't do at all, especially around Josh.

She did the only thing she could and turned deliberately away from Noah to face another one of the problems they'd managed to keep from him. "Yes?"

Noah was sure he should have heard the other man approach. Once again, though, the minute Dulcy had shown up, he'd completely lost direction. Instead of watching the carmine glow of the sunset, he'd been noticing how the red-gold tendrils of her hair tended to curl when they got damp, especially alongside her ears. Delicate ears. Soft hair, escaping that utilitarian braid so that it clung to her throat. Delicate throat.

There was nothing soft about her now, though. She'd gone right on point the minute the man had appeared out of the dusk to face off with them.

"I'm goin' to town," he challenged from ten feet away, his voice tight and raspy. "Okay with you?"

This undercurrent Noah couldn't miss. The man seemed to be Dulcy's age, but his good-looking blond features lacked the kind of defining edge Noah had grown accustomed to in the people of the valley. His chin was a little weak, his eyes a little close together. They were hot eyes, shifting and unsettled as he challenged a woman whom he outweighed by at least sixty pounds.

Dulcy straightened, her jaw working almost imperceptibly. "Your work done for the day, Josh?"

"You're not going to fault me on my work" was the only answer she got.

Dulcy just nodded. The ranch hand spun on his heel and stomped off. It was only then that Noah realized he was the same man who had made the crack that morning about what

Dulcy really wanted to do. The one Hank had shut up with no more than a look.

The man, come to think of it, who had most frequently taken Noah up on drink offers the night before.

Dulcy had already turned back to the house.

"He a long-time hand?" Noah asked quietly.

Dulcy looked over at him, and he could see how hard she was fighting to remain calm. "You could say that," she said. "Sorry I didn't introduce you, but he isn't any happier to see you here than he is to see me."

"Why?"

She grinned, but Noah saw the sadness, the stress, the wearing at her edges of what had gone on in this valley. "You bought the ranch from Cordelia Winters."

Noah nodded. "Yes."

"Josh is her son."

Ah. "And she didn't sell it to him?"

Dulcy shrugged. "He couldn't afford it. He worked for her just like any of the other men. Aunt Cordelia has never believed in coddling her children."

He should have known. "Aunt Cordelia?"

A grin, even a small one, eased the strain on her face. "Guess we forgot to mention that one too, huh?"

"I guess you did. How did *you* get the job?"

Dulcy shrugged, kept walking. "I'm a lot tougher than Josh."

"*Age of Innocence,*" Sally announced with a sweep of her hand.

Dulcy couldn't believe her eyes. In all the years she'd either visited the ranch or worked there, she'd never once broken bread in the dining room. Until the day she'd sold out lock, stock and barrel and moved to the big city—that being Billings—Aunt Cordelia had evidently lived her entire life without meeting someone worthy of her dining room table, because all meals had been prepared and eaten in the kitchen. Sally had obviously decided to change history.

"Sally, we've been branding cattle," Dulcy protested, wiping her hands against her pants in a futile gesture to press her rumpled clothing into service.

Sally was, as usual, completely unruffled. "And you changed your clothes an hour ago. I know, because I have them in my wash machine. And I'm sure you're hungry."

With that, she set the steaming roast on the table and turned back through the kitchen door for more food. That left Dulcy staring at her aunt's high-walled dining room with no little ambivalence. The faded rose wallpaper was familiar, the gleaming mahogany clawfoot table and chairs and lowboy. What made it surreal were the ivory linen tablecloth and silver candlesticks and good china that had gone with the sale of the house.

Another man's inheritance now. Another man's treasures.

"Isn't it lovely?" Hannah demanded from where she already stood by a chair, her brown eyes bright. "I set the table."

Noah pulled off his hat and grinned. "Looks great."

"We *never* eat here," Hannah confided, patting at the table as if it were a well-trained pet. "I think we should celebrate. I'll play for you."

Dulcy almost laughed out loud at the look on Noah's face. "The piano, maybe?" she asked, ruffling her daughter's hair.

Hannah's face fell for an instant, and then, ever practical, she nodded. "The violin," she announced. "Because my fingers still aren't long enough for something appropriate on the piano."

Noah smiled. "I would be honored."

"It'll be just like *Age of Innocence*," Sally reasserted, reappearing to set out the potatoes.

"It will be nothing like *Age of Innocence*," Dulcy assured her, standing in the door to the hallway as if she were still ten and had to be invited into the adults' presence.

Alongside, Noah stood silently, hat in hand, a hand up to rub at his still-dusty hair. The high sun had begun to bronze his face, and there were a few new lines at the corners of his eyes. Laugh lines, squint lines from looking hard into a flat, glaring afternoon. Honest lines.

"Of course it is," Sally challenged, handing off a steaming platter of carrots and turning back into the kitchen. "They ate a lot on good tables, and so are we. And since we can't have Daniel Day-Lewis, we'll just have to settle for Noah."

Dulcy laughed at Noah's nonplussed expression.

"Sally speaks in 'movie,'" she said simply. "You'll get used to it."

"Oh, by the way," Sally announced on the run. "Noah, your business manager called. Everything's arranged. That make sense to you?"

Noah nodded. "It means I can devote my full attention to the ranch."

Dulcy hoped he missed the look she and Sally shared. She hoped he didn't hear her heart start up.

"Well, it's not a postcard," Sally urged with a push to Dulcy's rump. "Come on, Hannah. Teach these adults how to enjoy dinner."

Hannah stood with her head cocked and her hands on her hips. "Nobody eats at my table without washing their hands first," she said in perfect imitation of her mother.

"Young lady—"

"Cleanliness is next to godliness, my mother used to say," Noah answered with a grin. "Wanna show me where, Hannah? And you can tell me where to hang my hat, too."

The two walked out the door together, Noah in his worn work clothes and battered boots, hat in hand like a gentleman caller, Hannah in her very best ruffled cotton blouse and Sunday skirt, her hair brushed into a gleaming riot. Dulcy felt like the dowdy stepsister.

She almost forgot that Sally was watching alongside. "Makes me think reading about movie stars is a waste of time." Sally all but sighed.

Dulcy shot her a look of surprise.

Sally just grinned. "Cameron Ross may be nice to fantasize about, but this guy's the real thing, Dulcy. And although I will deny I said it if I'm ever in Cameron Ross's presence, this guy's also better looking."

"This guy's the boss."

"And the boss is single, handsome, sweet and hardworking. Kind of like Forrest Gump with a post-grad degree and better bone structure. Life could be worse."

"It'll get worse if he finds out I've been lying to him."

"Make sure you don't. Otherwise, Hannah's going to be washing her hands back in Billings. Now, come on. Eat your dinner. I missed 'Entertainment Tonight' to cook it."

Finally Dulcy could grin. "Life as we know it may cease to exist."

Sally refused to be intimidated. "I'll have you know that there's some very interesting news afoot, speaking of Cameron Ross. He has gone to his island."

"Uh-huh."

"Alone. Don't you want to find out why?"

"No."

"Of course you do. No man who's just gotten engaged to the sexiest French actress since Catherine Deneuve goes off alone to do six weeks of *Robinson Crusoe*."

"I thought you said he always did this."

"Sure. Twice a year, without fail. It gets him away from all the attention. Nothing like your own island to keep away the riffraff. The helicopters spotted him yesterday. Maybe in the nude." Sally's eyes lit with imagination.

"What's nude?" Noah asked, on them before Dulcy could react. Face gleaming, hair damp, eyes bright.

"Cameron Ross," Sally informed him with some consideration. "You tell me. If you were engaged to Isabelle Renoult, would you go off on your own for six weeks?"

His reaction was microscopic. A tiny tremor along his jaw. A subtle dimming of the spark in his eyes. And yet, it was there, and suddenly Dulcy realized just what it was that had made Noah Campbell late to get there.

Evidently so did Sally. "Food's getting cold," she announced with another abrupt shove in the right direction. "And my own dinner's waiting for me. Let's go."

There was a certain amount of uncomfortable shuffling around the room and a second or two of taut silence, before Hannah commanded everyone's attention by waiting alongside her chair for the services of a gentleman.

"You may seat me," she informed Noah with demure eyes. "I hear that's how it's done."

"Not in this house," Dulcy informed the girl in a mother's tone.

"My house," Noah retorted with an easy smile. "My rules. And I think Hannah's right. Dining rooms deserve good manners." He gave Dulcy an assessing glance that edged her temperature up a couple of degrees. "Seems to me you haven't washed your hands yet, young lady."

Dulcy was feeling more disoriented by the minute. This new, very disturbing man in this old, very familiar room. Her much-too-adult and tomboy daughter dressed up as if for the White Rabbit's tea party, and Dulcy thinking of buns and thighs for the first time in almost seven years.

It was going to be a very long six weeks. Maybe the longest of her life.

She went and washed her hands.

# Four

Noah couldn't shake the feeling of unreality, as if he were playing a scene in one of his movies. He found himself sitting in a completely furnished dining room in his completely furnished house that had come with a temporary family, and they were eating dinner as if this happened every night.

Somebody should say something, like "Isn't this weird?" Somebody should take note of the fact that none of them belonged at this ironed and gleaming table with its fresh-cut flowers and sparkling crystal.

Somebody could have even mentioned the fact that after sharing meals with some of the more notorious beauties in the world, Noah shouldn't have been so taken with a scrawny, guileless woman with manure on her boots and a six-year-old she still hadn't explained.

Somebody should. But Noah, distracted by the sight of autumn red hair and flashing eyes, seduced by the almost hallucinogenic sense of family, knew he wasn't going to be the one to do it.

"So," he said instead, for once at a loss for easy conversation. "How long did you work for your aunt?"

Dulcy didn't even bother to look up from the pork roast she was unselfconsciously devouring. "About a year. Aunt Cordelia never did get along with the other ranchers in the valley. I was just another little burr under their saddles."

Noah almost forgot the food on his own plate. "You didn't mind?"

"Why should I mind?"

"She enjoys being a burr," Hannah piped up from her place across from her mother.

Dulcy gave a wry chuckle. "Thank you for the character analysis, Hannah."

Hannah stiffened a little. "Well, you said—"

"Yep, I sure did. But it doesn't mean you have to repeat it every chance you get."

Noah couldn't help but smile. They were so easy together. He envied them both. He ached, suddenly, for a scene like this he could really feel a part of, instead of observe as a visitor.

"You're a burr, too, Mr. Campbell," Hannah spoke up.

Noah blinked. "I am?"

Dulcy grinned. "Aunt Cordelia delighted in selling the place to you. It meant she didn't have to sell it to one of her neighbors. Or, God forbid, one of her kin."

"You're kidding."

"You weren't even the high bid on the place."

"Who was?"

Dulcy shrugged. "Who knows? That was part of Aunt Cordelia's fun. She just let everybody know she'd sold to a stranger for less money than she'd been offered by other people."

"Nice lady."

"A surprise in every package."

"And you had to live here with her?"

Hannah laughed. Dulcy grimaced. "Uh, no. We lived in the foreman's house."

Noah let an eyebrow slide north.

"It smelled," Hannah proclaimed.

Dulcy went back to her meal. "Just because she hired me didn't mean she liked me any more than she did Uncle Mike or Walt Stewart. We moved up here when she moved out."

Noah couldn't help it. "Just kind of took over, huh?"

Dulcy was grinning back, her eyes bright. "It's what you pay me for, boss."

"Evidently."

She chuckled. "If you want, we'll camp out while you're here. Seems an awful lot of trouble, though."

Noah had been so involved in the challenge in Dulcy's eyes that he'd forgotten the little girl sitting on the other side of the table.

"You're not going to make us move back, are you?" Hannah demanded, her voice suddenly small and uncertain.

Dulcy reached across to take her daughter's hand. "Hannah..."

The perfect truth was that Noah spent a fraction of a moment considering it. He'd come here for peace. He wasn't at all sure he was going to get any peace with Dulcy McCann under the same roof, reminding him at every turn just why he'd bought the ranch. With whom he'd planned to share it.

But to be perfectly honest, he sincerely doubted he'd get any peace no matter where she was on the ranch.

"Please," Hannah begged. "It scares me."

"No," Noah assured her as quickly as he could. "Of course not. I mean, if you moved down there, who'd play the piano for me?"

He knew he'd been taken when Hannah's expression went from desolate to exultant in the space of a heartbeat. It didn't seem to matter. He was going to let her get away with it.

"Should I play now?" she asked. "It helps the digestion, you know."

"You're kidding," he retorted. "It didn't help my digestion any when I had to play."

It was Hannah's turn to admit surprise. "You play the violin?"

"The piano," he admitted sheepishly. "I'm not that good."

Hannah waved aside his disclaimer, her eyes alight again. "You can accompany me," she decided. "Mom doesn't play anything but a lariat and her nose."

"Her nose."

This time the little girl giggled. "She says it's cheaper than a mouth harp."

Noah took a look at the sparkle in Dulcy's eyes and laughed. "And here Ethan said I'd be bored in Montana."

Hannah did play for them on the violin, a petite instrument for a petite girl, who somehow got sweet music from it. Dulcy found herself watching Noah watch Hannah. He didn't just endure it, he enjoyed it. He seemed to know where the music was going, and appreciate how Hannah sent it there.

Dulcy was jealous. If there was one thing she would change in her life, it was the fact that God had failed to give her the ear to appreciate the miracles her daughter was performing. She knew without having to ask that Noah had that ear and more. It made her wonder just what kind of piano he played.

She was still wondering when she came back down from tucking Hannah into bed to find him holding that miniaturized violin in his hand as if trying to decipher its mysteries.

"You weren't just being a mother," he admitted with a genuine smile as he set the violin back into the case and followed her into the kitchen. "She really does have talent."

"That's what I keep hearing," Dulcy said, setting the last of the dinner dishes in the sink. "All I know is that it's hell being intimidated by a six-year-old's command of music."

"Yeah, but you know more about bulls than any woman *I've* ever met."

Dulcy grinned. "I know what to do with them, anyway. You want that tour now? I usually do a last check before bed, anyway."

Noah took in the pile of pots and pans scattered over most of the kitchen surfaces. "Shouldn't we clean up?"

Dulcy snorted unkindly and walked over to retrieve her hat from the rack. "Sally wants to fix fancy food, let her clean it up."

If Noah was going to see the ranch, he had to follow her out the door. That was precisely what he did.

Outside, the sky was midnight velvet, strung with stars like a broken necklace. The air was clean and sweet with the smell of freshly cut clover, and the trees whispered with a late breeze. Without waiting for Noah to catch up, Dulcy set off for the outbuildings and paddocks where some of the stock dozed in the soft starlight.

"We have two separate animal barns," she said as she walked. "One for the horses, one for the cattle who need it. We also have shelters farther out for wintering. With what you pay for your cattle, you don't really want them lost out in the mountains when it snows."

"Of course not."

The only lights here came from the dawn-to-dusk lighting around the outbuildings, a rectangle or two from the house and bunkhouse. No city, no neon or helicopters or police cars. The only sounds Dulcy could hear were the dogs in the valley trying to outdo a coyote, a bell or two tied to the throat of an animal, and the steady wash of night wind through the trees. She wondered whether Noah would notice. Whether he would realize how magic it was.

She wondered whether he would love this valley as much as she did.

"Where's the herd now?" he asked.

"Summer pasture. The day before we brand our herd, we do Cletus's along the west fence. It's a smaller ranch, so most of our hands will be out bringing our herd to the corrals."

"Still at about three hundred units?"

Dulcy looked over, not sure whether his command of the situation made her feel better or worse. A unit comprised of a cow and her calf. Three hundred calves. A big ranch. A big responsibility.

"Yep. You'll be introduced to most of them in a few days."

She thought Noah would follow her into the barns. Instead, he wandered over to the nearest fence, where he could see out over the valley and the horses and cattle penned there.

"You have some of the cattle here," he said. "Why?"

Dulcy joined him at the rail fence. "Medical problems that don't do well on the range. We get a certain number of cases of mastitis every year. The mother has to be separated and treated, and the calf hand fed or enticed onto somebody else's teat if he's not old enough to wean."

Noah looked over at her, surprised. "You do that on a ranch this size?"

Dulcy knew she should keep her mind on calves and feed and milk. She couldn't seem to pull her attention away from those soft, clear eyes of his, though. The roughened angles of his jaw, darkened now with that incipient beard. The sense of energy he radiated, even leaning his forearms against a paddock fence and staring into the night.

Before she'd met Noah Campbell, she'd wanted him to remain an absent landlord, so she could run the ranch. So she could almost imagine it to be hers.

Suddenly, in the dusk, with his eyes half in shadow and his hands resting alongside hers on the fence, she wanted more. She wanted him to join himself to this land.

She *wanted* him to see in it what she did.

Dulcy hoped like hell he didn't hear her drag in that very unsteady breath. "You have prize cattle here," she said. "I don't like to lose any of them." Then she turned away to see those white faces in the darkness. "Besides, if you lived with Hannah, you wouldn't be able to let a calf starve to death, either."

Noah's chuckle was earthy, familiar, easy. Dulcy wanted to rub it over her skin like a rough towel. "How does she stand sending them away? Doesn't she know what you raise them for?"

"Sure. But it's easier to pretend they're at a cattle playground when they're gone."

"Of course."

They just stood there a moment, side by side, resting against the wood and watching the Herefords sleep in the dark. Comfortable. Companionable. Easy.

Dulcy could almost imagine that they did this every night. Saw the ranch to sleep together, protecting it from all the predators out there, both four-legged and two-legged.

She could almost imagine that he had already decided, once and for all, to let her belong here.

"Dulcy?"

"Mmmm."

"Is that calf walking backward?"

Dulcy grinned. "That's Wrong Way Corrigan."

"He's really walking backward?"

He was walking backward toward them. He must have heard Dulcy's voice and responded, just the way he always did. Wrong Way was a sucker for a scratched ear and a few senseless compliments.

Dulcy squatted down to where she could reach him when he backed against the fence and turned his pretty white face to her.

"He has pink eye," she explained to Noah, who towered over the two of them. "It was so bad we had to sew his eyes shut. It took him about ten minutes to figure out that it hurt less to back into barbed wire than shove his face in. Now he walks backward."

Wrong Way bawled, a high, mournful little sound that reminded Dulcy of nothing so much as Hannah whining for attention. Dulcy scratched.

Noah joined them, so that his bent knee slid along the inside of hers. "Well, I'll be damned. It's like having a two-hundred-pound golden retriever."

He reached out then, too, his hand tentative, his face relaxed and smiling. Dulcy looked at his hand. Chafed and a little blistered from the hard day's work, dark against the calf's white, white coat. Flat, square nails and big knuckles. Workman's hands. Perfectly tended workman's nails.

"Your hands got pretty beat up today," she mused. "Can't get a manicure out here, ya know."

Noah pulled his hand back to examine it himself. "Yeah, they're never going to be the same after this."

"Is that going to be a problem?"

He allowed one eyebrow to lift. "Nobody's checked my hands since Sister Pancretia in sixth grade."

Dulcy grinned again. She was always grinning around him. "Sally says that well-tended hands are important in big business. At least, they are in the movie business, which is what she's conversant with."

"Well then, I guess I should be glad I'm just a manufacturer, huh?"

"A manufacturer and a rancher," Dulcy amended for him.

For some reason her words touched him. She could see it in the sudden stillness in his eyes. In the shifting of posture and the quick duck of his head.

"Thank you," he said. "I take that as a compliment."

"That's how it was given."

Noah nodded again, his eyes up to the night, his thoughts once again his own. Without saying another word, he got to his feet. Dulcy gave Wrong Way a final pat before joining him.

"How far does the ranch extend?" he asked suddenly.

Dulcy turned to find him at a dead stop some ten feet away. His head was back, his hat off, his eyes out to the sky and the faint glow of snow on the Absarokas in the distance.

Dulcy couldn't see Noah's expression. Somehow, though, she knew what he was feeling. She could sense it, like a sympathetic resonance in her own chest. It was calling to him, seducing him, compelling him. It was beginning to wrap itself around him like a voluptuous woman, and he didn't stand a chance.

At least, she hoped not.

My God, she thought, stunned. His eyes were glistening. Glistening, as if they carried more there than calm consideration.

She could see the edge of his jaw in the faint light, could see the hollows of his cheeks and the way the breeze tugged at his hair. She could see that his eyes were half-closed, as if the valley were best felt and smelled and heard.

Dulcy had seen men curse in this valley. She'd seen them fight and struggle and defend. She'd never yet seen one fall in love.

"It's a hard place," she said, anyway.

Noah looked down at her, and she thought for just a second how his eyes were as ghostly pale as that distant, moon-touched snow.

"Trying to scare me off?"

"Making sure you understand. A lot of people have come to these mountains. A lot of people have left."

It was so quiet, suddenly, as if even the wind had died in anticipation. Dulcy felt her heart kick in again, painful and hard. Anticipating his answer, dreading it, no matter what it was, because suddenly things had changed again.

"Especially the greenhorns?" Noah asked gently.

She just shrugged, trying so hard to remain passive.

His smile, when it came, was slow. Pure. Bright in the darkness, as if it swelled from someplace inside and simply spilled out.

"Most greenhorns didn't have the manager I do" was all he said.

Dulcy heard more. She heard words he wouldn't allow himself to say yet. Words he wasn't allowed to share. She heard a current in that voice that bespoke secrets she had no party to.

She heard yearning and determination and dreams, and they all somehow revolved around standing in the darkness of a Montana night, talking about land and animals and survival.

And she didn't know how to answer.

She did the only thing she could. "Want to see the horses first?"

Noah grinned. "I'd love to see the horses."


Noah woke slowly the next morning and got out of bed even more slowly. He had expected to hurt. He hadn't expected to feel as if he'd just been dragged behind a car. He ate breakfast this time, knowing perfectly well he wasn't going to last another long day without food in his stomach, and he blessed Sally all over again when she medicated him with aspirin for his aches and coffee for his thick head. And then, just like the day before, he rode out with the hands to brand cattle.

This time they did the Flying Diamond, where Walt Stewart raised Simmental cattle and some of the best quarter horses in the state. It was a well-run ranch, with newly painted outbuildings and straight fences, and branding went without a hitch.

By the time they got to Mike Murphy's Triple M on the third day, Noah had had the chance to try his hand at almost all the work being done and was looked to as just another rancher in the valley. He walked away from the day more sore and tired and elated than he had in the past ten years.

Then he reached home and realized that Hannah was practicing.

Dulcy came upon him as he stood in the side yard considering his options.

"You want her to stop?"

He looked over at Dulcy and thought how much she had already become part of his life. How Hannah had brightened his mornings with her insouciance and charm.

"No. I think this might be a good time for me to take a ride across the ranch, though."

Dulcy's face folded into concern. "I can't go with you right now, I'm afraid. I need to run into the vet's for my supplies and then get a part for the harvester. Want to come to town?"

Noah shook his head. "You never answered my question the other night. Just how far can I ride and stay on Lazy V property?"

Dulcy pulled off her hat and pushed a few damp tendrils of hair from her dust-covered forehead. "You can just about ride all day," she said. "See the foothills across the river over there?"

Noah followed the generous arc of her hand to where it pointed beyond the Bitter River at the far end of the valley from the ranchhouse. Beyond, the land rose in a pine and aspen field that beckoned, cool and dark and mysterious, up to the rocky slopes of the closest mountains.

"Those my trees?" he asked, a little chagrined by the almost childish enthusiasm in his voice.

Dulcy must have heard it, too, because she smiled. "When I have the time, I'll ride most of the property with you. You'll see it goes a pretty good distance in that direction. Beyond that slope are two more before you reach real high country. A lot of the wintering cattle are tucked into those folds. The summer ranges are back up behind the house in those hills. You'll see that when we move the cattle up next week. But if you want to cross the Bitter over there, you'll see the trail in the trees. Follow that, and you can't go wrong."

Noah nodded, smiled. "See you for dinner."

It only took him ten minutes to saddle Doofus for the ride up. Noah was even more tired today than he had been before, since he'd done a lot more actual cattle wrestling. It didn't matter. He needed to get some space between himself and the other occupants of his ranch, and he couldn't think of a better way of doing it.

By the time Noah led Doofus from the barn, both Dulcy and the old battered pickup truck were gone. There were still odd-enough sounds emitting from the house that Doofus pricked his ears and whuffled. Hank had a couple of the hands working on repairing the outbuilding that held the farm equipment, and a couple more were putting away newly delivered feed.

The ranch was running smoothly, just as it had since Noah had bought it four months ago. Just as it had since Dulcy had taken over as manager.

Noah couldn't ask for more. It was everything he'd held in his imagination all those years. It was more. So much more.

He thought about that as he mounted Doofus and turned him out toward the open valley. He thought about it as they first cantered and then flat-out galloped in the late-afternoon sun that was gilding the western slopes and glinting off the river.

He was alone. No press, no fans, no business types who only wanted to help his career, no sycophants just wanting his business, his attention, his time.

Alone. Bent over a fast horse, riding across the land he'd busted his butt to get. The land he could call home. The land he could cultivate and protect and hand down to his children.

His children.

Children like Hannah, maybe, bright and inquisitive and unpredictable. Amazing individuals in spite of their parents' stamp.

Hannah had her mother in her. Not her eyes, those were probably her father's . . . whoever her father was. No, Dulcy lived all over again in Hannah's smile, brilliant and sudden and brash. In that particular coin of her hair, a gold-red that defied description, that pulled your eye to it with its unexpected depths and hues. She looked back out from that expression of confidence, that no-nonsense view of the world.

Dulcy lived on in Hannah's hugs and her memories.

Noah ached with unexpected yearning. The yearning he'd pushed down for so long. The hunger to belong, just like he seemed to in his dining room, in his kitchen after meals when they all gathered to do the dishes and dab soap suds on noses and toss dishes as if it were a carnival sport.

He longed, suddenly, not simply to be able to return to this ranch, but to return to this ranch as it was now.

He wanted it to be not only his home, but his family.

Damn, he needed to talk to Ethan. To measure this against his cousin's amazing pragmatism. He needed Ethan to remind him that he knew perfectly well he'd expected to bring Isabelle here. To see her eyes light with the discovery of these mountains, these wind-swept spaces.

To see his children grow in her, to be passed the gift of her beauty, her talent, her perceptive, insightful mind.

By now, Noah should have known better than dream dreams like that. He was in this alone. Probably for good. He needed the person he loved to love him here. As he was, without artifice. But the minute a woman found out about Cameron Ross, Noah Campbell was never enough.

And he couldn't be Cameron Ross.

He wasn't.

He stopped for a minute on the trail to turn and look back at the valley. His ranch lay there, spread out along the folds of the eastern edge like a model he might have put together on his living room floor as a boy. The white, big-porched house, as pristine and perfect as a man could envision, with eyelet lace curtains puffing out the bedroom windows with the wind, the tree swing out front and the garage to the side, all ringed by cottonwood and elms. Down the hill a little, the red outbuildings and barns, the animals meandering over the grass, the miles of fence, white and tidy all the way out to the main road where the gatepost boasted that this was the Lazy V Ranch.

Noah looked down on it and smiled and continued on up through the trees.

If this was all he could have, he'd take it. He'd take the wide open spaces, the normal life, the hard, satisfying work. He'd be more than happy to take the neighborly interest and unconcerned opinions and mundane routine.

Noah didn't know how long he rode. He really didn't pay attention to where he was, except for the fact that the path was getting steep and winding, and that he'd lost track of the house. He watched the blue of the sky deepen and the lazy afternoon clouds bump against the nearing mountains. He listened to the brush of the wind and heard a moose calling somewhere for its mate.

He began, for the first time in ten years, to relax and enjoy what he had. He began for the first time in his life to toy with the idea that what he had accomplished was a good thing. He was feeling so good in fact, that when disaster struck, it caught him unprepared.

Something punched him in the arm. Noah cursed, looked down at it, not sure what he expected to see. Almost instantaneously, he heard the first crack, and Doofus screamed. The horse reared up, and Noah went down.

He still hadn't figured out what had happened when he hit the ground head first and blacked out.

# Five

"**I**'m hungry."

Dulcy didn't even bother to look up from the repairs she and Hank were making on one of the stalls. "Honey, there's nothing I can do about it."

Hannah kicked at the dirt. "You can eat without him."

"No I can't. Now, why don't you go on out and keep an eye out for him. He should be coming back across the river anytime now."

"It's dark," Hannah objected, the level of her voice nearing a whine. "I can't see that far."

That made Dulcy look up. She hadn't really noticed. The rectangle of sky she could see outside the barn door had indeed darkened into that beautiful intense peacock in which floated the first stars. Even with Bart busy at his weekly poker night, Sally would still be chomping at the bit to get home. There was a special tonight on the gossip channel about the state of the royal family.

And Hannah was right. It was way past time to eat. Dulcy's stomach was aching like a sore tooth for the chicken she could smell. The bunkhouse had been served, and now it was her turn.

Except that she couldn't really eat without Noah there.

"You don't think he got lost, do ya?" Hank asked without noticeable worry.

Dulcy sighed. "Nah. He's been chompin' at the bit to get out there since he showed up. Probably lost track of time. It's not really dark. Hannah's just bein' a kid."

"A *hungry* kid," her daughter amended.

"Have a banana," Dulcy retorted, just as she always did.

"Eeew," Hannah flashed back the standard response as she clomped on out of the barn door.

"Think this'll hold?" Hank was asking of their handiwork.

Dulcy straightened from where she'd been bent over the hinge they'd jury-rigged and stretched, a hand to her aching back. "It'll have to. I'm tired and I want a bath. We'll have Billy get a new hinge in town tomorrow."

She bent to gather up the tools they'd used.

"Mom! Mo-o-o-om! I see Doofus!"

Dulcy pulled her hat off one of the posts and plopped it on her head as she turned for the tack room. "Good, honey. Why don't you tell Sally? And wash your hands."

"Guess the bath'll have to wait," Hank offered dryly.

Dulcy grinned. "Just till I get my stomach to stop growling."

"Mom!"

That was a different sound altogether. Dulcy didn't even bother to drop her tools. She just spun around the other way and headed for the sound of her daughter's frantic call. Hank followed hot on her heels.

"Hannah?"

That was when Dulcy heard the hoofbeats. Fast, hard. She got outside in time to see Doofus run straight for her tiny daughter.

"Hannah!"

But that wasn't what had scared Hannah. The tiny girl simply lifted her hands and brought the horse to a stuttering halt inches from her nose. Dulcy could see the white of the horse's eyes, saw the sweat on his flanks.

Saw, most importantly, that his saddle was empty.

She slowed to a halt. "Damn. He did get lost."

Hank chuckled. "Looks like old Doof dumped him after all."

Which meant that after a grueling day at Uncle Mike's, a trip into town and a host of other small details to tend to, Dulcy was going to have to put off her dinner even longer while she saddled up a horse and went looking for her wayward boss in the dark.

She called him the worst name she could think of and headed on into the barn and lifted a saddle off the rack. "I'll saddle up Colorado, Hank. Would you get Buster ready to take along so the boss doesn't have to walk back? I don't think Doof's in the mood to be a gentleman."

"Yeah . . ."

Dulcy was already in the stall, slipping a saddle blanket on the back of her horse, when she heard Hank's hesitation.

"Boss, I think you'd better see this."

She just took horse and tack out with her. "What?"

Hank didn't look happy. Dulcy found out why when he turned to her and lifted his hand. On his fingers was something dark and shiny and wet.

Dulcy came to a stop. "What is it?"

"Blood. I think the boss did more'n fall off."

Dulcy had never saddled a horse so fast in her life.

Colorado, infected by Doofus's nerves and Dulcy's urgency, danced around in the barnyard as Dulcy gave his cinch a final yank and pulled him around to mount him. Hank let Hannah take temporary control of Doofus so he could help.

"Get the others," Dulcy commanded as she launched herself into the saddle. "Follow me up. And bring the cellular, just in case we need help. Hannah, let Aunt Sally know."

"Mommy, I can't," Hannah protested, her young voice frantic. "Doofus is hurt."

Dulcy paused just a moment to verify it with Hank. The older man nodded, no longer looking very sanguine about the whole thing at all. "Pretty sure it's just a nick, but all the blood isn't from the horse. Go on."

Dulcy wheeled her own horse around and took off across the valley.

She was glad she'd decided to take Colorado. The big Appaloosa was as surefooted as a cat in the rocky high country. He never faltered as he carried Dulcy to the river and beyond to the other side of the broad, broad valley Noah seemed to love. Toward the trees he had been so delighted to call his own.

Up into them, the shadows deepening in the dusk until Dulcy could barely see. Slowing now, even as she checked back and saw the flickering lights of sudden activity back at the ranch building. Hoping against hope to come across Noah as he walked back down the trail. Hoping they were wrong, that Doof had just dumped him and hurt himself hurtling back to the ranch for the dinner he'd been due, too.

Frantic. Nothing more constructive. Mouthing an amorphous prayer that everything was all right. That nothing had happened to Noah up here on the steepening rocky ground in the dark.

He was the boss, after all. Dulcy was dependant on him. They all were. He held their futures in his hands, and if something happened to him, they'd all be in trouble.

She'd be in trouble.

Oh, God, if something happened to him.

Dulcy didn't want to think about the fact that the fear that bubbled up beneath those very logical words had nothing to do with job security. It had nothing to do with anybody else on the ranch. Even Sally.

Even Hannah.

It had to do with that flashing, surprising smile. That ear for music and the perfect manners with a proper little girl.

It had to do with the surprising gleam of tears she'd caught when he'd looked up toward these very hills on another dark night.

"Noah!" she yelled, startling Colorado into almost losing his footing. "Noah Campbell, are you up here?"

All she heard were the pines, the skitter of the quaking aspen in the night breeze. The chirrup and chatter of birds settling for the night, and animals waking to the hunt.

She heard, far across the valley, an engine starting up.

"Noah!"

Nothing.

Dulcy rode on, fighting the urge to hurry. The last thing either of them would need would be for her to steer her horse right over him if he'd landed on the ground.

"Noah!"

He had to be here somewhere. She'd told him to take the trail. To just follow the trail up as far as it would go.

He hadn't promised he'd do it.

If he wasn't on the trail, she might never find him.

"Noah!"

"There you are."

Dulcy almost fell off her horse. "Noah?"

She couldn't see him.

"Up here."

She kicked Colorado hard and sent him skittering up the slope. It wasn't until she was almost on Noah that she saw his shadow.

"Noah? Are you all right?"

He was sitting on a boulder. She could tell by his shadow, the darkness now almost complete up here on the west side of the valley.

"I'm fine," he answered easily. "You?"

That did it. Dulcy swung off her horse and stalked over to him. Tried like hell to see past the crooked grin and tilted head to what had left him sitting on a rock in the dark when his horse was a couple miles away.

"What the hell are you doing up here?" she demanded, relieved and angry and hurt at the same time. "Hannah thinks you're dead! What happened to Doofus?"

If he'd deliberately tried, Noah couldn't have made her more angry. His grin grew even bigger. "Is this how mothers say 'I'm glad you're okay'?"

Dulcy wanted to hit him. "Next time you decide to send your horse on alone, pin a note to his saddle blanket so we don't have to come crashing up here in the dark. All right?"

"Is he okay?" Noah asked. "The last time I saw him I was somersaulting backward. He didn't wait around to explain."

"He's bleeding."

"I was afraid of that."

Dulcy dragged in a shaky breath. She just wasn't ready for him to be so damn nonchalant about this, after she'd been getting ready to airlift him to Billings. "What happened?"

Noah didn't seem particularly concerned. "I must resemble an elk. Doof and I were just walking along minding our own business, when somebody tried to make us hood ornaments. Doof bolted, and I ended up on foot."

"And just sat here on a rock waiting for us to show up?"

"No. I was walking down. When I realized you were coming up, I figured it would be prudent to just sit out of the way and wait. After all, I'd already had one person not realize there was a human in the area, and look what that did for me."

"Did you see who it was?"

Dulcy could see him shake his head. "Uh, no. I kind of hit my head on the way down. It took a little while for me to remember who *I* was."

That quickly, the sense of relief fled. "You hit your head?" she demanded. "Where? Is it all right? What else did you hurt?"

As if it were an answer in itself, Noah levered himself to his feet. "Dulcy. I'm fine. I'm hungry. Can we go now?"

"Nothing else is hurt?" she repeated, needing his denial more than she wanted to admit. Fighting for the first time in too long the urge to reach out and touch a grown man, if only to reassure herself.

"Nothing important. Besides, I'm hungry, and I'll bet you guys ate all the chicken before I could get back."

"We did not eat the chicken," she protested. "We were waiting for you."

"Then let's go."

Dulcy glared up at him for a moment, unable to tell anything with his hat shading his face into anonymity and his dark shirt and jeans hiding anything else. She just wanted to know he was all right. For the moment, she couldn't think past that.

"You can ride behind me," she finally offered, turning back to her horse.

"A pleasure."

Colorado was still a little skittish, so that it took Dulcy a second to pull Noah up behind her. When she did, she heard him grunt, as if he were more sore than he was admitting. She was about to mention it, when he wrapped his arms around her waist.

Thought fled.

Dulcy froze.

Somewhere she knew that they had to get moving. They had to get back down to where the rest of the ranch was probably even now spilling across the meadow in a concerted rescue effort. She had to get them both some food, because why else would she be so suddenly light-headed?

"Dulcy?"

"Huh?"

"What's wrong?"

Noah's voice, right in her ear. His breath, fanning her cheek, igniting some weird glow in her stomach. He was so big, wrapping completely around her. If he wanted, he could just fold her completely to him. He could tilt her head back and kiss her with his soft mouth and mystic eyes and chiseled jaw . . .

This was stupid.

Childish.

Hormonal.

Dulcy knew better. She still couldn't breathe.

"Dulcy?"

Did he sound breathless, too? Was he holding her just a little more tightly? His lips were so close to her ear that just that one word spilled shivers all down the side of her neck. His hands were stiff against her waist.

"Yes?"

"We need . . . uh . . ." Softer this time. More hesitant, the words fading away to soft breath, his face against her hair. Folded close, his chest against her back. His thighs alongside hers.

"To get, uh, back," she agreed with a tiny nod of her head. "Yeah."

But if she moved, she'd bump into him. She'd stoke that odd, dancing fire that licked along her limbs like heat lightning.

She felt him dip his head, felt his lips edging closer to her skin, to the exquisitely tender skin at the nape of her neck.

"Dulcy?"

Her eyes were closed now. Her heart was thundering. "Mmmm."

"What's wrong with *me?*"

He was smiling. She could feel it all the way to her toes. She could have told him what was wrong with him, if she could have breathed.

She couldn't.

"Hey, boss!"

The two of them jolted apart so fast they almost fell off the horse.

It was only then Dulcy heard the clatter of horses approaching up the slope. The whole ranch must have, indeed, turned out.

Even before Dulcy could master a command, Colorado turned himself down toward his stablemates and whinnied. Probably disgusted with humans as a whole.

Dulcy could hardly blame him. She was sure pretty disgusted with herself. God, she'd come so close to stupidity. Her body was still shaking with surprise, with something else she didn't even want to deal with right then.

"Right here, Hank!" she yelled back, her voice as unsteady as her heartrate.

"Find him?"

She didn't need to answer. Everybody saw that she had, when they broke through the last of the trees. Dulcy just let Colorado continue his descent.

Hank pulled up within a few feet and considered Noah with a wry eye. "First you get my men drunk, then you get my horse shot. What's next?"

"He okay?" Noah asked.

At the sound of his voice, Dulcy almost turned on him. How could he sound so normal? So...unflustered? She still felt as if she'd run up on her legs instead of Colorado's. Noah sounded as if they were conversing at a bar.

"He's fine," Hank acknowledged. The rest of the men just waited behind him, their horses snorting and stamping a little, kind of like an equine Greek chorus. "You?"

"Need dinner. We ready to go?"

"Brought you a horse. You still want it?"

"No," he said.

"Yes," Dulcy said at the exact same moment.

She saw the eyebrows raise. She ignored them. "We'll make better time."

Noah couldn't seem to come up with further objection. It took him a second to slide off and then climb on Barney, but in the end he took up his place in line in front of Dulcy, and everybody turned back toward the ranch.

As they started off, Hank pulled up alongside Dulcy on the trail. "You want me to...?" His focus strayed back up the mountain.

Still too rattled to think well, Dulcy just shook her head. "Tomorrow. It's too dark now."

Hank just nodded and eased back into line, leaving Dulcy with too many uncomfortable thoughts. It wasn't simply what had happened up on that trail, but what could have happened. What she'd wanted to happen. Dulcy didn't want to think of it. She knew she'd have to deal with it in the light of day, but till then, she thought she'd just concentrate on getting downhill.

She'd just be glad Noah was all right.

If only it were that easy.

It was getting dark, and the moon was rising over the Absarokas, spilling silver into the valley. A coyote tested the darkness, and a couple of the horses nickered. Other than that all was still. Peaceful and dark and magic, just as Dulcy usually liked it.

Not tonight. Tonight she couldn't seem to hear the night sounds or feel the wind. She couldn't even enjoy Colorado's easy gait under her. She couldn't seem to move past that very surprising contact on the slope.

Electric.

Seismic.

Over.

There was just no way she was going to allow herself to turn into *Tammy and the Millionaire* when so much depended on her keeping her job. She wasn't going to let herself get involved with Noah, or worry about him, or wonder what would have happened if Hank hadn't shown up when he did. The old saying about what else you shouldn't get with your paycheck was true for too many good reasons.

It might have worked if she hadn't bumped into Noah as they were all dismounting. Noah flinched and set off more than one alarm bell.

Dulcy turned on him to see that he was trying very hard to hide the hand he was using to shield his left arm. Worry flared right back up like a trick birthday candle.

"Noah?" she asked, turning her attention to that dark blue shirt that seemed suspiciously moist in the yard light. "What's wrong?"

"I'm hungry," he insisted, heading toward the house.

For once Dulcy let Hank take care of her horse for her. After all, she figured, if she let something happen to the boss, they'd both be out of a job.

"How 'bout if I check your arm?" she asked, reaching out.

Noah danced away like one of the skittish horses, his eyes glinting oddly in the light, his right hand still around his left arm.

"It's nothing," he insisted.

"Maybe," she said. "But it's bleeding."

He faltered to a stop, his sudden grin lopsided and endearing. "I know. But I didn't want them to," he admitted, motioning toward where the men were leading their horses into the barn. "I don't want them to know what a wimp I am."

Dulcy let an eyebrow lift. "A wimp."

"It's a scratch . . ."

"And a smack on the head," she reminded him.

His shrug was embarrassed and uncomfortable. "I'm trying hard not to be a greenhorn, Dulcy."

Dulcy couldn't help it. She laughed. She shook her head and took gentle hold of her boss by the arm and guided him toward the house. "Cowboys fall off their horses all the time," she assured him.

"But they don't complain when it hurts."

She laughed again. "You've been watching too many old Marlboro commercials. They whine louder'n a two-legged dog trying to hit a hydrant. Now, come on and let's look at that."

Just shy of the back door, he came to a sudden stop. "Dulcy, about what happened up there."

Dulcy looked him right in the eye and thought herself the bravest woman on earth for not crumbling on the spot. He towered over her, his eyes almost glowing down at her with their moonstruck silver, his hair tumbling over his forehead like a little boy's. She couldn't lose her heart to this man.

She wouldn't.

He wasn't smiling. Dulcy wanted so very badly to lift a hand to that bristly cheek and soothe the worry lines. She wanted to produce that quick, flashing smile.

She didn't. She did probably the hardest thing she'd ever done in her life, when she'd done many hard things.

"Up there?" she asked, her voice deceptively certain, so there would be no mistake. "Nothing happened up there."

And then she turned from him and walked in the door.

# Six

"That's a gunshot wound," Sally pronounced, rag poised over Noah's arm. "You out robbin' banks again?"

Noah did his best to grin. "How you think I bought this place?"

"Oh, that," she scoffed, tipping a bottle of hydrogen peroxide over the rag and slapping the whole mess against the gash in his arm and stoking the fire all over again. "I thought you did that by legal robbery."

Noah did his best to keep quiet and smile. "Thanks."

"He gonna live?" Dulcy demanded as she walked back in the house from where she'd been putting her horse away.

Noah couldn't believe it. How could she seem so matter-of-fact, as if nothing had happened? Had he imagined it? Had he been hit so hard on the head that his entire body had shortcircuited right into putting his nose into her hair?

He felt as if he'd been struck by lightning.

He felt . . . he felt . . .

God, it was a good thing he was the actor and not the screenwriter. The truth was, he didn't know how the hell he felt.

KATHLEEN KORBEL                      71

Surprised and antsy and upended. Distracted as a teenager getting his first look at a naked girl.

In all his life he'd never used anything but the gray matter between his ears to guide his actions.

There had been another guide entirely, out on that trail tonight.

There was another guide now, even though he knew perfectly well there was some other cerebral business that had not yet been attended to. A quick, muttered conversation he'd almost missed entirely.

"He's gonna live," Sally assured his manager. "Is Hannah ever coming back in from the barn?"

Dulcy tossed her hat on the rack and walked over to the coffeepot. "Nope. She finished her dinner and took her stuffed bear and her violin to soothe Doofus to sleep. She also has her sleeping bag out there in case he should wake during the night and cry out in pain."

Noah almost forgot what Sally was doing to his arm. "I didn't think he was that bad."

"His scratch is smaller than yours. But Hannah worries about her friends."

"This is not a scratch," Noah protested, lifting his arm for her to see.

It was a scratch, but it was throbbing and almost as sore as his head, and he thought he deserved at least as much concern as a horse.

Dulcy stopped right alongside him and bent for a close inspection. Noah was sure she meant to be funny. The minute her hair got in proximity to his nose, he knew she'd blown it.

She'd been out in the dirt all day, wearing a ten-year-old hat in eighty-degree weather while wrestling a couple hundred calves. How the hell could her hair smell like oranges? Noah wanted to drop his head into it again and never come out.

"You must be a greenhorn," she teased, straightening as if she couldn't read his thoughts. "Cowboys are never this lucky."

Noah scowled. "Thanks."

"How's your head?"

"His head?" Sally demanded, back on alert.

"He hit his head when Doofus decided to come home without him," Dulcy said. "Didn't he show you that, too?"

"So I could do what?" Sally countered. "Kiss it and make it better?"

Noah caught Dulcy's faint blush. He saw her eyes flicker his way and then shy away again. He knew just what she was thinking, because he was thinking the same thing. About what he'd like her to kiss and make better.

God, he had to get a handle on himself. He'd come here for some rest, and right now it looked like he wasn't going to sleep for the next six weeks.

Not only that, but if he gave action to any of the thoughts that were plaguing him, he'd be without a foreman, fast. And he didn't want that.

He didn't want that at all.

"Coffee?" Dulcy asked abruptly, stalking back to the pot.

"Thanks."

"So, how *is* your head?" Sally demanded, wrapping gauze around his arm.

"Sore." Confused, confounded.

"You dizzy? Faint? Seeing double?"

"Not since I sat down on the trail."

Sally spent a second peering at him, as if she could see his brains through the hair on his head.

"I'm all right," he insisted, even though he really didn't feel like it. But that wasn't something he could discuss with either of these women. Not now, at any rate.

Sally didn't seem to believe him. Instead she laid a hand on the back of his head and made him wince.

"That's a hell of a bump."

"It wasn't so bad until you slammed into it," he protested, pulling her hand away.

"Even so," she insisted. "You should be careful. Somebody should keep an eye on you."

"I told you, Sally," he insisted. "I'm fine. I used to do this all the time when I . . ."

"When you what? Worked a rodeo?"

No, he thought with some chagrin. When he'd worked as a stuntman on his way up. He'd almost told them both the truth, which just went to show how this place was beginning to affect him. How these people were affecting him.

"When I worked on my uncle's ranch. I used to help him work the new horses, which meant I spent a lot of time flying through the air. And hitting my head. It doesn't feel any worse."

He could tell she still didn't believe him. Nothing much he could do about it. Slapping one last bit of tape on the bandage on his arm, she collected her supplies and headed back for the bathroom.

"So that's why you're so good on a horse," Dulcy suggested, setting down his coffee.

He nodded and lied through his teeth. "That's it. I counted every day I could during school until I could get to vacation and the ranch."

"Did you grow up in Texas?" she asked.

He nodded, another lie. All lies, just like everywhere else in his life. Except for how he felt about this place. About that poor, dirt and scrub ranch he'd worked all those summers. "My whole life," he said. "Philadelphia's just where I landed."

"*Witness,*" Sally inexplicably piped up as she walked back in the room.

Dulcy glared. "He already told you he's okay, Sal. And besides. I don't see you bathing wounds by lantern light."

Sally headed straight for the cabinets and began pulling out dishes. "Not me," was all she said.

Noah could have sworn Dulcy blushed again. Come to think of it, so did he.

Then Dulcy punctuated the conversation as only she could. "I also think Harrison Ford wouldn't have fallen off his horse in the first place."

"He fell off his car," Sally insisted. "And he owns a ranch."

Noah checked Dulcy for an explanation for Sally's logic, but she just shrugged. "Well, that makes all the difference in the world. I'm gonna wash up for dinner. I assume we're still having dinner?"

Sally set the dishes down on the table and turned back to her heap of pots and pans. "Dry chicken, overcooked string beans, and potato pellets. Coming right up."

Still feeling a little queasy from all the extracurricular activity, Noah just sat at the table. "You two sure seem to know a lot about movies," he ventured carefully, testing waters he knew he shouldn't.

Setting down a couple of aspirin to go with his coffee, Sally laughed. "We *one*," she amended. "I'm the videophile. Dulcy puts up with it because she can't cook."

"You can't cook?" he called out to where he could hear water splashing in the bathroom. "You're kidding!"

"The last time I checked," Dulcy retorted easily, "the job description for a ranch manager does not include having a secret recipe for apple pie."

"Wouldn't hurt."

Sally waved him off as she proceeded to set the table around him. "Don't get her started. She'll tell us all—in much too much detail—the things she can do that I can't. Most of which involve sliding entire arms into pregnant cows."

"*City Slickers*," Noah couldn't help but offer with a grin.

Sally brightened immediately. "See? You can catch the hang of it pretty quickly. You don't go to movies?"

He saw the quick flash of uncertainty in her expression when she said that, as if she knew she'd said something that didn't make sense. As if she couldn't quite figure out what it was yet.

He wondered how long it would take her. How long it would take any of them.

Noah wondered, sitting in the warm peace of that kitchen with the sounds of crickets and coyotes drifting in the window and Vince Gill on the radio, how much longer he'd be able to hide out and pretend he could be the person he really was.

He'd invented himself for Hollywood. He'd done too good a job of it all round.

"No," he said, looking down to consider the coffee in his cup and telling the best truth he could. "I don't really get much time to go to the movies."

Which was true. If he saw them, he saw them in somebody's private screening room.

"You should go with us," Sally suggested. "Or we could rent a movie or two. You should see something with Cameron Ross. Did I tell you that you look like him?"

Noah hadn't won the Oscar because people liked the color of his hair. He sipped easily at his coffee and flashed Sally a grin, even as his heart did a two-step that would have left old Vince Gill gasping. "You already have the job," he said dryly. "You don't need to push it."

"No, really," she insisted, not looking at him anymore as she served up what looked nothing like overcooked or dried out anything. "You weren't really born in England, were you? If you were, you could be brothers."

"Sorry to disappoint you. Is he still on the island?"

Sally simply scooped up a couple of tabloids on the way over to the table. "See for yourself. I still want to know where Isabelle Renoult is."

Noah had been about to pick up the top of the pile when Sally's words brought him up short.

Isabelle.

There she was, her picture superimposed over the shot of the island compound, with Cameron Ross chipping golf balls alongside a palm tree. Noah had forgotten how beautiful she was. Sleek, sensual, lithe as a cat.

Different.

It seemed almost as if he didn't recognize her anymore. As if what he'd seen in her wasn't there, maybe had never been there. Maybe he'd imposed on her the very same impossible ideal she'd imposed on him. Suddenly, though, she looked shallow. Cold. Intelligent rather than intense.

Four days, and Noah was disconcerted to find that all that slick sophistication had attracted the myth he'd created, not the person he'd rediscovered here in the mountains.

Not two months ago, he'd told a respected journalist that he couldn't imagine his life without Isabelle. Now, in the space of three days, he couldn't imagine it with her.

"What do you think he does all day?" Sally asked, leaning over his shoulder.

Noah startled all over again. "Who?"

She pointed to the suntanned, muscular image of a screen star, his teeth gleaming, his hair tousled to perfection. Noah scowled. He was going to have to have a word with Ethan. He was beginning to play Cameron just a little too well.

But then, if he fired his cousin, who was going to provide his diversion when he wanted to escape?

"Looks like he plays golf," he said.

"Can't be any fun just doing that," Dulcy offered, plopping down in the other chair.

"Sean Connery seems to like it," Sally retorted.

"Sean Connery's over sixty. Golf is boring. Which means, I guess, that Cameron Ross is boring, too."

Dulcy had just picked up the plate of chicken to serve herself. Sally snatched it out of her hand with a scowl. "You wouldn't say that if you'd met him," she challenged, making it a point to hand the platter to Noah instead.

Noah almost missed the plate entirely. "You've met Cameron Ross?"

Thank God, she blushed and shook her head. "No. But my friend Patsy from the junior college did. She was right in the front row outside at the Oscars this year. Almost got to shake his hand."

"Makes your heart just want to stop beating, doesn't it?" Dulcy drawled.

Sally glared a little more. "Cameron Ross is suave, sophisticated, brilliant and solves crime in a tux. You got a problem with that?"

"Cameron Ross solves crime in a tux?" Noah couldn't help but echo. "Must cut into his acting schedule."

"And play hell with his cleaning bill," Dulcy added.

"*Man on the Run* and *Second Agenda*," Sally said in a kind of wistful voice Noah knew only too well. "He makes James Bond look like a slacker in a Sears suit, and Dulcy's not impressed. But then, Dulcy writes fan letters to Hootie and the Blowfish . . . whatever the heck that is."

Noah wasn't ever going to get his food. "You *write* them?"

It was Dulcy's turn to squirm. "For Hannah. She's nuts about their music."

"And you don't listen at all."

She shrugged. "Just a little."

Noah couldn't help it. He let out a laugh they should have heard in the bunkhouse. "Hootie and the Blowfish," he marveled with a shake of his head.

"Okay," she retorted, "so it's not opera. It's—"

"One of my favorite groups," he informed her.

That brought the kitchen to a dead halt. Sally was still standing by the table with the potatoes now clutched to her chest as if needing protection. Dulcy sat with her fork halfway to the chicken, staring at Noah as if he'd told her he worshipped Satan.

"Oh, come on," she objected.

"To be specific," he amended, taking the potatoes from an unprotesting Sally, "my favorite group is the Crash Test Dummies. But I'm real fond of Hootie. Not to mention Green Day and Shakespeare's Sister and the Cranberries, and... well, I enjoy the new alternative music almost as much as Hannah. In fact, the one extravagance I did indulge in is a stereo system that should be showing up soon with my CD collection."

He could see that he still hadn't quite convinced them.

"But I thought you'd, well, you know..."

"Live and breathe the classics? Hardly."

"But when I called, your business manager was always saying you were at the opera. Or the symphony. Or the ballet. I just figured..."

Ah, Ethan. Always ready with an alibi if anybody should try and get in touch with Noah. Ethan, who in Philadelphia ran Noah's commercial investments. Who worked as the blind for the various persons Noah was. If Hollywood wanted Cameron Ross during an "island vacation," Ethan, the faithful business manager, either rerouted the call or took the message. The same for the other side, where Noah Campbell was really the silent partner in The Campbell Group that Ethan had started on Noah's money and run on Ethan's acumen.

Ethan looked enough like Noah to stand in for him at a distance, like now on the island, and sounded enough like him to filter off annoying problems. Ethan was the single person in the world who knew all of Noah's secrets. Who had sat out on that fire escape with him, weaving plans from dreams, and now celebrated their realization.

"Yes," Noah finally said. "I was at all those things. Fundraisers. Tough to raise money for hospital wings at black-tie Hootie concerts, ya know?"

Dulcy actually groaned. "Oh, God, I'll never hear the end of it now."

Sally seemed to be enjoying Dulcy's distress. "Well, the old ranch just isn't going to be the same anymore, is it?"

"If she were dead, Aunt Cordelia would be rolling in her grave," Dulcy assured them.

"I wouldn't count on it," Sally countered. "I think she's rolling right now... oh, damn. *Witness!*"

Noah noticed that Dulcy was once again as confused as he was, so he just waited.

Sally swung her arm in the direction of the phone. "The Tiltons called. The barn raising's scheduled for the end of the week. Can you make it?"

Back on familiar turf, Dulcy took a second to actually dispatch some food. "Yeah. We should be finished by then. Wanna come, boss? There's a dance afterward."

Noah's first instinct was to say no. He was getting comfortable around the men, but then, men weren't usually the sex that recognized him first in the grocery store.

Still, he'd fooled Sally, and he figured that there wasn't a bigger Cameron Ross fan in the state. He might as well dip his toes into the social pool and see if he liked the water.

See if the water liked him.

Besides, he was intrigued by the idea of being out on a barn floor with Dulcy in his arms.

"Sounds great. Do I bring my own tool belt?"

"Just your sparkling personality."

Moving among laughing, talking strangers to the sound of slide guitars, colored lights strung around the barn, his hands around her waist, her hair thick and loose around her shoulders.

"What about you?" he asked. "Are you going to be there?"

Dulcy grinned. "I'm a whiz with a band saw."

Red and gold and honey, shimmering in the strung lights, her soft gray eyes languid with the music and the movement.

"What about the dance?"

This time she looked a little more disconcerted. "Sure. I guess."

"In a dress?"

That endearing pink crept up her throat. "I own a dress."

From over by the sink, Sally hooted. "Which you haven't worn since Hannah was baptized."

"I'd like to see you in a dress," Noah said before he thought about it.

For a second the air in the room seemed to freeze. Dulcy's eyes grew infinitesimally bigger, and her breathing stilled. Then, as quickly as she'd stopped, she moved again. Flashed him a sassy grin and went back to her food.

"Better'n seein' *you* in a dress," she said, and Noah laughed.

The night was almost perfectly still. Straight up in the sky the moon melted the stars, and above the meadows, the pines whispered like conspirators. When she opened the door to the horse barn, Dulcy heard the horses shift and settle. She inhaled their earthy scent and let her eyes get accustomed to the shadows.

She still felt as if she were hooked up to electricity. It had been over two hours since she'd sat at the table with Noah, and she still couldn't settle down.

A barn dance. She'd been to dozens. Usually spent her time at the punch bowl with the other foremen, watching contentedly as Hannah and her girlfriends taught the boys to dance. She exchanged gossip with the people who did talk to her and ignored the slights of those who wouldn't. Dulcy attended out of a sense of loyalty to her community and neighbors. She hadn't really anticipated one since she'd been in high school.

She wasn't really sure anticipation was what she felt now. Maybe dread was a better word. Or ambivalence. It was the strangest thing. When Noah had asked her about a dress, Dulcy could have sworn she'd felt his hands at her waist. Felt her cheek against his shoulder, the air moving against her legs as the two of them glided together across a floor, their heels clacking on wood, their words as whispered as the pines.

She could have sworn he'd felt it, too.

This had to stop. She didn't have the time for this. She didn't have the patience. She certainly didn't have the fortitude. If anyone in this valley caught on to the fact that she was attracted to the new owner of the Lazy V, the rest of her already tattered reputation would be no more than shreds.

Not that she hadn't survived it before. She had. But before Hannah had been too little to understand. Hannah had not been in school with the children of spiteful people who would bring that spite intact to class.

And Dulcy simply would not do that to the little girl she found curled up and asleep in the end stall.

"Hey, Doofus," she crooned when the horse lifted his head in greeting. "She taking care of you?"

Doofus butted her on the shoulder and then dipped his head so she could scratch his ears. Dulcy watched her little girl sleep, one arm around her bear, the other around the battered violin case with its music school and Pearl Jam stickers.

It made Dulcy want to cry. It made her pray that she would never again make the kind of mistake that had brought her little girl into her life, because if she were that stupid again, she'd ruin Hannah's life.

"She's beautiful."

Dulcy jumped back as if she'd been hit.

How could she have not heard him? How could she have not felt him following her down the hill?

Because she was still so rattled after that conversation she'd had at dinner, she wouldn't have felt a UFO land on her roof and shut down the electricity for the state.

She felt him now. Briefly Dulcy closed her eyes against the sudden surge of delight that threatened to swamp her.

"Come to apologize to your horse?" she asked.

He walked right up next to her and did his own scratching. Doofus didn't seem to mind the extra attention at all. "It wasn't my fault."

"Horses are not notoriously good at discriminating things like that."

His smile was so beautiful. Rough and easy and right.

And then he blew it. "Wanna tell me what was going on up there this afternoon?"

Dulcy looked over to find him still intent on the horse. "You tell me," she said carefully. "I was just the cleanup squad."

Then Noah looked over at her, and Dulcy knew she had a whole other problem on her hands. "What was Hank going to go look for?"

"Hank?"

"You told him to wait till tomorrow."

"Ah." Dulcy did her best to think fast. She looked back down at Hannah, as if afraid of waking her. Knowing perfectly well that if Doofus stepped square on her daughter's chest it wouldn't even alter her breathing.

Just what should she tell him? How much would he accept?

How long would she have before he found out his staff was conspiring behind his back?

No wonder she felt so at sea. Not one terrifying secret on her hands, but, it seemed, hundreds.

"He was going to see if he could find out who fired at you."

"Why? I told you. I thought it was a hunter."

Dulcy faced him then. "Uh, it isn't season right now."

"So, what? Poachers?"

She shrugged. "Maybe. Maybe... uh, neighbors."

That did seem to stop him. Noah took his own look down at Hannah, then at Dulcy, and suddenly his eyes were darker. Sharper, as if his brain had been on vacation until that moment. "That's a comforting thought."

"You weren't the only person who bid on this property, ya know."

"I know."

"The last thing several people wanted was for an outsider to take it over."

"No surprise."

"Well, some of the less rational might just feel that a... well, a warning might be called for."

"You're kidding."

She shrugged again. "I was going to say something after Hank got back tomorrow. Like maybe you should only go out riding with one of us with you."

His eyes widened. "You're serious."

"I don't want to lose you," she blurted out. "I mean..."

Dulcy could feel the flush climb her throat. She could feel the sweat pop up on her palms. The last thing she'd meant to do was tell him the truth. The last thing she needed on this earth was for him to suspect.

"I mean," she said before he had a chance to interrupt. "That nobody else in this valley would have let me stay on here. And if I don't work here, I can't afford those trumpet lessons for Hannah."

Dulcy couldn't even look at him anymore. Couldn't raise her gaze above the level of about the third button on his dark blue shirt. Even that was bad enough, because it allowed her to see the fact that he seemed to be having as much trouble breathing as she.

"Well, we wouldn't want that to happen," he murmured, his voice suddenly tight.

"No," Dulcy said. "We wouldn't."

"I mean, who else would I be able to share my Hootie and the Blowfish CDs with?"

"Exactly."

"And there wouldn't be anybody to pull Hannah's chair out at dinner."

It was getting even more difficult to breathe. "True."

"And if I left," he said, reaching out a hand to lift her face to him, "I'd never get the chance to see you in a dress."

That did it. Dulcy stopped breathing altogether. She stopped thinking. All she could comprehend was the fact that his eyes seemed alight, pale as the moon-washed sky, sweet as the water that tumbled over mountain fields.

She heard his breath catch, a harsh sound that shuddered through her. She felt the tremble of his fingers where they rested beneath her chin.

Dulcy wished she could say that Noah kissed *her*. That he took advantage of her. She wished she could lay the blame for what happened at his feet.

She couldn't.

Somehow, the two of them met in the middle. Noah dipped his face to hers so that his hair spilled over his forehead and his eyes closed and his whiskers tickled her cheek. Dulcy raised up on her toes until her breasts brushed against his chest and her hands somehow found his shoulders.

Until her mouth met his.

She'd been kissed before. She'd been thoroughly loved, once upon a time when it had all still seemed magical and true. She'd never dipped her fingers into lightning. She'd never lost her way simply at the touch of a man's lips.

But she did. Oh, she did. Standing there amid the horses, not five feet from where her daughter slept. She forgot them all, forgot her past and her future and her problems. For a brief, explosive moment, she found herself trapped in a whirlwind and unable to break free. For a heartbeat, it didn't matter, and she was happy.

# Seven

And then, damned if she hadn't just walked away. Just pulled back, her eyes still huge and moist and heartbreakingly hurt, shaken her head and walked out the door.

And Noah had been too much of a coward to follow her.

He was too much of a coward *now*. If he weren't, he would be out at Cletus Wilson's ranch working alongside her, instead of pulling the pickup into a parking slot in front of the feed store in Westridge.

He should have argued with her that morning when she'd told him she didn't want him risking his neck again this soon after his fall by branding Cletus's cattle or herding his own with the hands who were going to get ready for branding at the Lazy V the next day. He should have pulled rank, even though he had felt like hell.

Not from the fall—he'd taken worse in staged fights on movie sets—from the fact that he'd walked back into that silent, echoing house and lain awake the entire night. He'd watched the moon set and the valley slip into blackness, the stars finally getting their chance to shine through. He'd watched the sky ease from ebony to pearl to mauve to coral. He'd heard the birds wake and the animals rustle to life. He'd heard the alarm bells ring throughout the compound and Sally's car crunch across the dirt drive as she'd arrived to cook breakfast.

He'd lain in that bed the entire night sweating for a woman who slept no more than fifteen feet away.

And he hadn't done a damn thing about it.

Cameron Ross would have slipped to her door and whispered sweet nothings, making everything all right, earning him entry, winning him her smile and the sweet comfort of her body.

Cameron Ross would have had a script and a director and seventy crew members standing around waiting for break. He would have had Makeup spraying his hair into place and Wardrobe readjusting his silk boxers.

But he wasn't Cameron Ross. He was Noah Campbell, and Noah Campbell couldn't do those things.

Which was why he'd invented Cameron Ross in the first place.

"Mornin'. Aren't you the new owner of the Lazy V?"

Noah almost walked right by the man speaking to him. Smallish, balding, successful looking in a portly, well-fed way. Smiling like a salesman with his hand out.

"Morning," Noah responded, taking it out of courtesy.

"Name's Bob Grumman. First Montana Bank. Your loan's with us. Just wanted to welcome you to Westridge."

Noah let his smile grow. "Why, thank you. Noah Campbell. It's my pleasure to be here."

Bob Grumman was already nodding, as if he'd figured as much. "Woulda been out to the ranch right after branding, anyway, but since I'm here... Anything you need, sir. Anything at all. Can't tell you what it means to us for you to have kept that loan in town, when you could have taken it back east and all."

"Well," Noah said, "the Lazy V's part of Montana's economy, not Pennsylvania's."

That got him a hooting, happy laugh. "When's Hank takin' over for you?"

"Hank?"

"Foreman. Now that old lady Winters is outta there, we all figured..."

"Nope." Fingering his hat in a Western salute, Noah stepped up on the sidewalk. "Real nice meeting you, Bob. It's a pleasure working with your bank."

He met the same question in the feed store, the small appliance store and then in the little general store that looked so much like the one his aunt and uncle had owned in Dawsonville, Texas.

"Why not?" the proprietor asked as he rang up the food Sally had asked Noah to pick up while he was in town carrying out the duties of one of the men who'd been pulled to herd cattle. "Hank's a real good man."

"Dulcy seems like a real good woman," Noah said evenly.

His real answer came in the lift in the man's eyebrows. "You don't say."

It didn't take an interpreter to figure that one out. Only one reason to choose a woman over a man in these parts, the man implied. Noah objected even without the words.

"You stop that right now, Pete Dunn," a scrawny, sharp-eyed woman in a housedress said in protest, finger out toward the man behind the counter as she stalked up from the aisle where cereal was stuffed on shelves alongside canned vegetables and light bulbs. "I swear, you'll be flower fertilizer before you ever admit that women have the vote."

"It's not that, Vera, and you know it," he countered.

"Well then, there isn't anything else," she said with sharp finality. "You hear me?"

Noah turned on the woman and was rewarded by a smile. For the briefest of seconds he hesitated, wondering just who the smile was for. Wondering if he'd been caught after all.

He hadn't. She held out her hand. "I'm Vera Dunn," she said. "This Neanderthal's wife. And I'm real glad to see you aren't held back by some of the stupider notions that are so popular around here."

Noah shook her hand. "Noah Campbell. A real pleasure." This time he meant it.

She looked hard at him, but just for a second, as if trying to remember if she'd seen him in town. Noah held his breath. But before he could blow his own cover, the bell over the door tinkled and everybody's attention swerved.

Every one of Noah's alarm bells went off.

"Afternoon," Pete said, greeting the new pair of customers with the careful courtesy that had been Noah's first introduction.

"Hi, there," the woman answered with a five-hundred-watt smile. Salon-tousled blond hair, designer, stone-washed denim jumper and white T-shirt, silver-, and gold-studded lizard skin boots, surgery-enhanced everything. Accompanied by a six-foot, Nautilus-primed, airbrushed and Armani-draped vision in yellow sunglasses, thousand-dollar silk and sockless loafers.

Melanie Miller and Barry Feldman. Hottest husband-and-wife production and direction team on the continent. The hottest team Cameron Ross wouldn't work with, anyway. Noah would have compared them to sharks, but even sharks only fed when they were hungry.

Before they could figure out he wasn't just a local, Noah yanked out his shopping list and headed back for the cereal aisle.

"We're staying up at Jack Logan's place," Melanie was saying in her sharp, listen-to-me voice. "And thought we'd just pick up a couple of nice chards for dinner. We thought Chilean, but only because Jack hasn't even tried Chilean yet. Can you imagine?"

"No, ma'am, I sure can't," Pete answered in a drawl that halved his speaking speed.

Piling shredded wheat and lima beans into his arms, Noah grinned.

"We don't carry...chards," Vera continued. "We have some beer on the far aisle and cooking sherry by the window."

There was dead silence. Noah almost peeked over the top of the cookies to see the expressions on old Mel's and Barry's faces. Alongside them the bell tinkled again and a tiny, wizened lady struggled in the door without the two of them noticing. Vera swept right by them to give her a hand in.

"You're kidding," Melanie finally ventured to say. If Noah hadn't seen Barry screaming obscenities on a movie set, he would have sworn he never spoke.

"You might try Bozeman," Vera offered, busy patting the little lady on the arm as she went by. "I hear they got a gourmet place."

"Or Butte," Pete added.

"Billings," Noah couldn't help but add, knowing that only the top of his hat could be seen. "The Mystic Duck. They have great chards. And cabs."

"Really?" Melanie countered, obviously not hearing the sarcasm. "Is it far?"

"Couple of hours."

Another silence, this punctuated by the bell and more new footsteps.

"I don't suppose you have any tiramisu, either."

"Not unless it's got a Campbell's label on it," Pete assured her.

Noah kept his head down as he followed the sound of their foot steps and the opening door.

"I'm not living here in these conditions," Melanie was insisting.

The bell rang over the door, and Barry's distinctive growl could be heard for the first time. "Live here? Who says we're going to live here? At least not yet. You know what he said."

Noah came out of hiding to see the two of them conferring alongside their shining white Range Rover.

"There isn't anyplace called the Mystic Duck in Billings," Vera informed him without looking his way.

Noah laughed. "I know. But I figured all the fresh air'd do 'em good."

"What the hell *is* a chard?" Pete complained. "Damn if all those folk don't always come in here askin' for it."

"Wine," Vera told him. "Some kind of wine. So's cabs."

"Uh-huh. Why the hell don't they call it wine?"

"'Cause when you can afford lizard skin boots," Noah informed them both, "you figure you can afford something hottier than wine."

Vera sneaked him a look. "You don't drink chards?"

"Not unless I need to get drunk fast and there isn't any whiskey around."

"And who the hell's Jack Logan?" Pete demanded. "She said that like I should know. He didn't grow up here and I forgot, did he?"

At that, Vera sighed. "He's that movie star. The one who kicks people. He bought the Tyler place and closed all the roads up the mountain. Where you been?"

"Working here, woman."

"He bid on your place, too," she told Noah.

That got a nod out of Pete. "Good thing he didn't get it. Be a waste of a fine herd. Fine land. I swear, if one o' those Hollywood types showed up here actually wanting to do some ranching, I'd sell this store and walk the streets of Los Angeles with a sign that said I'm Sorry."

"Isn't that the truth," Noah agreed, thinking that Pete and his wife would never know what made him smile.

Pete was still crabbing about chards and tiramisus and things when Noah piled his entire cache on the counter to check out. By then a few other shoppers had entered, been introduced and sized up their new neighbor. Not one showed signs of recognition.

"Dulcy know where she's goin'?" One of the newcomers asked.

"She's not going anywhere," Vera answered for Noah as she settled the last of the groceries into his bags. "So just let everybody know."

The man nodded, eyes a little wide. Alongside him, the little old lady who had finally introduced herself as Miss Retta Williams, nodded with approval. "She was a good student," she said.

"She's a good girl," Vera insisted, as if it were an oft-quoted argument, then turned on Noah. "Well, you tell Dulcy if she needs anything, just let me know."

"I will."

"A spitfire of a girl. Especially after what she's been through."

"What she's been through," another voice interrupted disdainfully from a back aisle.

Noah caught Vera's scowl just before he turned to see who had just joined the party.

Another woman, this one plump and fair. She must have come in when he wasn't looking. Once pretty, Noah thought, but long since soured enough that all her lines seemed to curve down. Her mouth, her eyes, the lines at the corner of her nose

Thick dishwater hair swept into a roll and pricy slacks, a silk blouse and pearl earrings. Pushing fifty, at least physically. She glared at Vera as if facing off with a heretic.

"Now, Mary," Vera cautioned, hands up. "This isn't the time."

"And just when *is* the time, I ask you? You think this man doesn't deserve to know just who he has running that fancy ranch of his? I've been listening to you all skirting around things, and I've had it."

Noah held very still, just like old Pete over by the cash register. Except that Pete had a kind of anticipatory look in his eye, like he was getting the pay-channel fights for free.

"Dulcy's made her mistakes . . ." Vera started to say.

"Mistakes," the other woman hissed. "I'm tired o' hearing about 'mistakes.' Broke her father's heart, that's what she did, and him the best minister this town's seen. Broke his heart and sent him into exile." Without even drawing breath, she swung a finger around at Noah, as if he were a third-grader caught tossing spitballs. "You want her to run your ranch so bad? Just remember. Don't take your eyes off her."

"Mary!" Vera protested, aghast.

"Don't 'Mary' me!" she challenged. "It's *my* pearl necklace she stole."

"You don't—"

"I do. I did then and I do now. She'll fool you," she warned, pointing at Noah again. "Make you think she's sweet and dedicated and all. She'll steal from you, right under your nose."

"I know all about her," Noah lied, unable to listen to the spite pouring out of this woman's mouth.

"You do, do you?" she retorted, her eyes bright with self-righteous indignation. "Did you know that she's missing some of your cattle?"

"Come on, Mary," Pete finally spoke up. "We don't know for sure . . ."

But Mary only had eyes for Noah. She waved a finger at him again. "You *don't* know. Have her show you on that fancy computer she has. You'll see. A leopard doesn't change its spots. Don't take your eyes off her."

And then, without doing any of the shopping she must have come in for, she simply walked out the door.

For a minute there was a taut silence. Noah could almost hear his heart thunder. He just couldn't tell whether it was from outrage or fear. Missing cattle? What the hell was she talking about? And why did the whole damn valley know about it when he didn't?

"I'm so sorry, Mr. Campbell," Vera said. "You didn't need that on your first day in town."

Noah came very close to shaking his head to clear it. "She's sure been saving that all up to tell me."

"She's not a bad woman," Miss Retta said, excusing her. "She just never did really get over it, is all."

Over what? Noah could have asked, if he hadn't jumped in with that stupid lie.

"I'm sure," he said instead. "Must be hard on Dulcy."

Both of the women nodded, their expressions identical.

"That's why I think she deserves the break," Vera said. "She's never really had one from this town."

"But she stays here."

She shrugged. "It's home, isn't it?"

That simple. Noah ached suddenly to be able to say the same thing. To know one place so well he would defy everything to return to its comfort. To take the friendship of this place and these people for granted. To know he wouldn't have to sec- ond-guess the people around him, the people who worked for him, the woman he loved.

The woman he loved.

It wasn't something he could think about right now. Not when he could still feel the startling heat from Dulcy's kiss. Not when he'd stayed up all night fighting the absolutely insane notion that she was the person he'd wanted to fall in love with instead of Isabelle all along.

Because now, everything had changed again.

Noah was all set to ask Sally when he got back to the ranch. He didn't. He was set to ask Dulcy when she got back from her day, sweaty and dusty and exhausted. He was ready when he saw his herd penned up on the broad meadows alongside the buildings, ready to be branded.

How many were there, he wondered? How many were there supposed to be?

What exactly had Dulcy done in her past that had divided the town into camps?

But he didn't ask. He ate his dinner and paced his house and tried again to sleep under the same roof, and the next day, bright and early, he assumed his place among the men who gathered in the pearly, predawn mist to send his own cattle through the chutes. He worked with his hands and his arms and legs, that day, and let his mind take a break. He savored the sight of hundreds of glossy, white-faced Herefords, of the huge-eyed calves and placid mothers, of the well-trained horses and dogs, of cursing, laughing hands and bright sun. He lived the dream he'd dreamed for thirty years and forgot the questions.

And just as before, he watched Dulcy. Sharp, sensible, smiling Dulcy, who seemed to somehow grow more beautiful beneath the harsh sun, her braid halfway down her back and her nose freckled from the sun, her sleeves rolled up and her eyes seeing everything. He watched her and realized that not one of these men who worked alongside her realized what a treasure she was.

And he wondered why.

By the time they had the ranch to themselves again, the sun had set. The cattle were grazing back in the holding pens and the horses were bedded down. The trucks and trailers had departed, and the only sounds that could be heard were the cattle and the coyotes.

Unable to remain in the house with the sky such an incredible color, Noah took his coffee out on the porch and just sat. Just listened to the clatter of dishes from the kitchen, the murmur of voices as Sally and Hannah finished up, the creak of footsteps over old wooden floors. He watched the sun pull the gold and red from the sky and leave behind a deepening lapis, through which stars gathered in ever increasing clusters. He was tired and sore and sated with the feeling of hard, worthwhile work. He was trying his damnedest to ignore the sound of computer keys in the office Dulcy kept in what had once been the guest bedroom just above him.

Behind him, the screen door creaked and slammed.

"Oh..."

Hannah. She obviously hadn't expected him.

"Wanna sit?" he asked. "I'm trying to pick out constellations."

She didn't need to be asked twice. Taking a place next to him on the front steps, she tilted her head back. "You like watching the stars?"

"Yup. Don't get to see 'em as much where I live."

"You don't have stars in Philadelphia?"

"Too many lights."

"Oh. That's sad. Mom and I look at 'em all the time." She lifted a hand and pointed toward Orion's belt. "There's Phil."

"Phil?"

She giggled. "Phil the Amazing Sheep." She swung her arm further, closer to the Little Dipper. "And that's Bob the Bodacious Bunny, and Hannah's Harp."

"It is, huh?"

"Sure. They're my constellations. Mom gave 'em to me."

Noah found that instead of watching the sky, he was watching the child. And that the child had eyes that glowed bright with intelligence, like her mother's. "She did, huh?"

"Sure. We used to look up at 'em every night when I was very little. Mom told me all about what constellations were, and I asked her what their names were. So she told me."

"About Bob."

"Uh-huh. When I got older I found out that she didn't really know the constellations. She just made 'em up. I know all about Orion and Cassiopeia and all. But I like Bob and Hannah and Phil better."

Noah found himself nodding. "Yeah. Me, too." He found himself imagining Dulcy sitting alone in the night with a tiny girl in her lap weaving tales of magic animals in the sky and giggling, heads close together, their magic hair a dark fire in the dusk. He found himself unspeakably jealous of the two of them.

"Are you gonna make us move, Mr. Campbell?"

That brought Noah up with a start. "Why would I do that?"

"Because that's what the kids say."

Noah took a sip of his cooled coffee to cover his surprise. "Well, don't listen to everything kids say, Hannah."

She turned to him with a flashing smile, just like her mother's. "Well," she said. "I'm going to say good-night to Doofus."

"Say good-night for me."

And she was off the steps with a clatter, leaving Noah behind with more questions, fewer answers and a truckload of frustration.

"She giving you her 'poor orphans in a storm' routine?" he heard from behind him.

His heart jumped. He hadn't heard her coming down the stairs. Turning around, he saw her silhouetted by the living room lights, all shadow and no substance, just like him. "Not really," he admitted, trying to sound nonchalant. "She was teaching me about constellations."

The door creaked open again, a lazy, friendly sound Noah realized he'd missed in his years in L.A., and she joined him on the steps.

"It's always a challenge keeping up with her," Dulcy admitted, her own coffee cup dangling between her knees.

She had on jeans and a T-shirt, and tendrils of her hair curled over the milky skin of her neck. Noah didn't want to take his gaze from her. He did to save his sanity. "You do a good job of it."

"I have lots of help."

He didn't know what else to add. For a long time, they just sat there, side by side on the porch watching the night. Hannah raced back up the steps, plopping a kiss on her mother's cheek as she clomped on through into the house, and Sally headed out the same way, waving goodbye as she climbed into her little compact and turned for home. The night deepened and cooled, and still they didn't move.

"I think silence is highly underrated," Dulcy finally said.

Noah looked over in surprise. He was thinking the same thing.

"Good company makes all the difference," was all he could manage to say, aching as he was to own what they shared at that moment.

"You haven't asked," she said suddenly, still not looking at him.

"About what?"

"About what I'm sure you heard in town yesterday. I heard that Aunt Mary spilled her guts to you."

Noah couldn't hide his surprise. "She's your *aunt?*"

That actually got a smile from her. "Sure. Uncle Mike's wife. You think anybody else in this valley could afford pearls? Uncle Mike makes it, and Aunt Mary spends it. When she's not lecturing all of the rest of us on how to budget ourselves better, anyway."

"Where do they fit in on the family tree?"

"She's my dad's little sister . . . well, younger sister. Thanks for standing up for me."

"I had lots of help. Vera and Miss Retta."

Another smile, this one laced with nostalgia. "Oh, Miss Retta couldn't say anything bad about anybody if her life depended on it. But I understand you lied like a rug."

He wasn't sure what to do. What to say. "In a manner of speaking."

"It's no secret, Noah." She chuckled, a wry, knowing sound. "At least, not around here. I probably should have told you first, though."

"Want to tell me now?"

"I'd better. Otherwise, God knows what other lies you'll get caught in."

She was quiet for a moment longer, studying the far hills and listening, Noah thought, to old voices. "My dad is a good man," she began, oddly enough. "A minister with a true faith. Unfortunately, he had to have the bad luck to have more than one daughter, and the second one simply didn't turn out like he wanted."

Noah wondered what the hell he could have wanted that Dulcy wasn't. "What happened?" he asked instead.

"What happened?" She shrugged, a minute movement that spoke eloquently of her priorities. "Hannah happened. I'm afraid I've had an unfortunate tendency to buck the norm."

"So I've noticed."

She grimaced. "Thank you. The sad fact is that I was a notorious rebel in my teens. Nothing new or interesting. Ultrastraight parents, high standards and all. I'm ashamed to say that I lived up to every stereotype ever written about the minister's daughter."

"And Hannah's father?"

"Knew just what to do with a stereotype. He fulfilled every rebellious fantasy up to and almost including that old favorite, 'Take me away from all this.' The only thing he took away was himself. I was sixteen."

"What did your parents do?"

"What any good parents did. They sent me away. Actually, it was the best thing for everybody. They sent me to Sally's parents in Butte, who saw to it I finished high school."

"And they sent you to college?"

"Nope. Nobody had the money to send me through college."

"Then the agricultural degree is fake?"

That was the first thing that seemed to affront her. "It is not. I had a partial scholarship and worked the rest."

"And Hannah?"

"Went with me. Considering how she's turning out, I'm thinking about doing a paper on the effects of higher education on the minds of infants. She has a frightening store of information."

"Like Phil the Amazing Sheep."

This time when Dulcy smiled, it was the smile of a Madonna, and Noah found his objectivity slipping even more. "We used to sit in the window in this crummy little apartment I shared with a couple of other students and count the stars. Hannah was going to be an astronaut then." Her smile grew, softened even more. "And a ballerina. She was three."

Noah didn't know how to answer. What to offer in exchange. It occurred to him that for all his notoriety and success, he didn't have a tenth of this woman's strength. Her simple, straightforward courage. Noah hid behind layers of half truths about who he'd been and what he'd become. And he had less to really hide than she did. But she simply waded in and through and out the other side, as if that were the only thing imaginable to do.

"You didn't ask about the necklace," Dulcy admonished, surprising him all over again.

"I figured you'd tell me." At least he did now.

She sighed, and this time Noah felt real weight. "Suffice it to say that the money Aunt Mary thought I'd gotten from stealing her necklace was actually an under-the-table loan from my mom. My dad might be able to stand on principles about Hannah, but Mom had spent her whole life waiting to be a grandma.''

"And you don't know who stole it?''

"I didn't say that. I just said that I didn't.''

Nothing else to say.

What about the cattle? Noah wanted to ask. What else aren't you telling me that I'm seeing in the eyes of the people you know?

But he couldn't ask. He couldn't breach this tenuous connection with an accusation that might, somehow be true.

He couldn't even admit the fact that his trust had been affected by a bitter woman's accusations.

And an honest man's reaction.

So they sat together there in the night, sharing the silence and listening to their own thoughts. And all Noah could manage finally was the realization that in the still of the summer night, he could smell the soap on Dulcy's skin. A clean, soft scent that reminded him of breezes and high meadows.

She was like a wildflower, he thought. She looked so fragile, but she had a surprising strength. A tenacity to take root in hostile environs. Easily bruised, but so far never killed. A rare treasure that would never have survived the streets of L.A.

Noah had bought the ranch to realize a dream. Sitting next to this small woman with her unruly auburn hair and half-chewed fingernails, he was just beginning to realize what the dream was. And what it might, in the end, cost him.

He should have been asleep. He was tired enough. Battered and sore and worked like a stevedore. But two nights later he found himself wandering the rooms of the first floor after midnight trying to settle the storm inside. That was why he was awake when the phone rang.

"Noah?''

Noah plopped down on a kitchen chair. "Ethan? What the hell are you calling me at this hour for?''

There was a pause. A wry voice that sounded, he knew, an awful lot like his own. "I always call you at this hour. What's the matter, ranching making you a changed man?''

# NO COST! NO OBLIGATION TO BUY!
# NO PURCHASE NECESSARY!

# PLAY "LUCKY 7"
# AND GET FIVE FREE GIFTS!

# HOW TO PLAY:

1. With a coin, carefully scratch off the silver box at the right. Then check the claim chart to see what we have for you—FREE BOOKS and a gift—ALL YOURS! ALL FREE!

2. Send back this card and you'll receive brand-new Silhouette Desire® novels. These books have a cover price of $3.99 each, but they are yours to keep absolutely free.

3. There's no catch. You're under no obligation to buy anything. We charge nothing—ZERO—for your first shipment. And you don't have to make any minimum number of purchases—not even one!

4. The fact is thousands of readers enjoy receiving books by mail from the Silhouette Reader Service™ months before they're available in stores. They like the convenience of home delivery and they love our discount prices!

5. We hope that after receiving your free books you'll want to remain a subscriber. But the choice is yours—to continue or cancel, anytime at all! So why not take us up on our invitation, with no risk of any kind. You'll be glad you did!

NOT ACTUAL SIZE

*This beautiful porcelain box is topped with a lovely bouquet of porcelain flowers, perfect for holding rings, pins or other precious trinkets — and is yours absolutely free when you accept our no risk offer!*

# PLAY "LUCKY 7"

**Just scratch off the silver box with a coin.**
**Then check below to see the gifts you get.**

**YES!** I have scratched off the silver box. Please send me all the gifts for which I qualify. I understand I am under no obligation to purchase any books, as explained on the back and on the opposite page.

326 CIS A3JJ
(C-SIL-D-08/96)

NAME

ADDRESS                                                APT.

CITY                          PROVINCE            POSTAL CODE

| | |
|---|---|
| **7 7 7** | **WORTH FOUR FREE BOOKS PLUS A FREE PORCELAIN TRINKET BOX** |
| 🍒🍒🍒 | **WORTH THREE FREE BOOKS** |
| ⬭⬭⬭ | **WORTH TWO FREE BOOKS** |
| 🔔🔔🍒 | **WORTH ONE FREE BOOK** |

Offer limited to one per household and not valid to current Silhouette Desire® subscribers. All orders subject to approval.

© 1990 HARLEQUIN ENTERPRISES LIMITED          **PRINTED IN U.S.A.**

If offer card is missing, write to: Silhouette Reader Service, P.O. Box 609, Fort Erie, Ontario L2A 5X3

CDMA
Membre

019561919-L2A5X3-BR01

SILHOUETTE READER SERVICE
PO BOX 609
FORT ERIE ON    L2A 9Z9

MAIL▶POSTE
Canada Post Corporation/Société canadienne des postes

Postage paid    Port payé
If mailed in Canada    si posté au Canada

Business    Réponse
Reply    d'affaires

0195619199    01

"No. But you're going to wake Hannah."

"Hannah? Who's Hannah? That's awfully fast after Isabelle, isn't it?"

"Hannah is a six-year-old who happens to belong to the manager you contracted and never told me about."

"No kidding. Well, that's something else, then. . . ."

Noah suddenly forgot sleep and all the work that waited for him in the morning. "Something else?"

"Uh, yeah. I've been going over all the records from the ranch."

"You're on a tropical island with a houseful of servants, Ethan. It's supposed to be vacation."

"I'm on an island by myself, Noah. That's no vacation. So I brought my laptop and the modem, and pulled the ranch's info."

"Yeah?"

"Did you know that the books aren't balancing?"

# Eight

"**D**id you know your mother had legs?"

Dulcy glared at Sally with a little too much irritation for the harmless joke. "It's a dance, Sally," she snapped, wishing with all her heart she felt better. "Get over it."

Sally, darn it, laughed. "You look beautiful tonight, Dulcy," she said, mimicking her tone. "Live with it."

"You *do*," Hannah echoed, the sincere surprise in her voice betraying both her painful honesty and the truth of how Dulcy had been living since her daughter had been born.

"Thanks, Hannah," she retorted with a rub of her daughter's head. "Many more compliments like that, and I may just expire."

"*My Fair Lady*," Sally intoned.

Dulcy scowled mightily. "You're overplaying your hand, Sally."

Even so, Dulcy felt as much a charlatan as Eliza Doolittle must have felt at her first formal function. Not because Dulcy was trying to mold herself into something else. Because she wasn't sure just what she was supposed to be anymore. She'd become almost comfortable in her jeans and boots, as if they could protect her from the kinds of problems she'd been so prey to. She'd become asexual, almost invisible to the men who worked and cursed and fought alongside her without remembering she had breasts.

"This is stupid, Sally," she protested again, smoothing her hands along the flowing gauzy skirt. "I didn't need a new outfit."

Especially something with nothing more than a silk camisole and embroidered vest to go with the skirt. She didn't need to wear lipstick and eye shadow and mascara, either. She'd dug them out, anyway, along with her favorite old tortoiseshell combs to pull back her thick hair.

No braids tonight. Her hair was full and wavy against her shoulders. Dulcy ran her fingers through it, straightening it just like she did her clothes. She didn't know why. It wasn't like she was trying to impress her Uncle Mike or any of the hands.

It wasn't as if she wanted Noah to look at her differently.

To notice that she did have breasts.

It was just a stupid barn dance after a hard day out in the sun.

"This is worth the price of the ranch," she heard behind her and forgot every one of her objections.

Then she turned around and almost forgot her name.

He was just in jeans. Jeans and a soft white cotton shirt and gray jacket. His hair was still damp from the shower, and it curled at his neck. His beard was growing fast, making him look rakish and dangerous. His eyes...

His eyes settled on her in a way she hadn't wanted since she'd been sixteen. His smile was every fantasy she'd ever owned about a man, and it was making her knees weak.

"We ready to go?" she asked, her voice unforgivably breathless and her hands ironing the sides of her skirt.

He gave his head a slow shake. "I'll have to thank the Tiltons personally."

"Why?"

"For giving me the chance to find out that you have more in your closet than plaid shirts and boot-cut jeans."

Dulcy scowled, whirled around to leave. "You're as weird as Sally tonight." Her skirt followed her, brushing against her bare legs, whispering against her skin like a secret, and she remembered what was fun about wearing skirts.

She was almost out the door when he said something that stopped her in her tracks.

"*Man of the Hour*."

"Oh, my God," Sally breathed. "What a thought."

"Don't be silly," Dulcy scoffed.

Silly wasn't the word. Not for that movie. Even Dulcy had seen it, dragged by Sally in a moment of weakness when the bad weather had kept the work at a minimum and the cabin fever at a fever pitch.

*Man of the Hour*, Cameron Ross's latest movie about a con man posing as a European prince, who ends up making the glittering, beautiful and lonely queen of a fictitious country fall in love with him. The movie had sported more diamonds than a baseball league, more tuxes than an Italian restaurant, more class than...more class than Dulcy had seen in one place in her life. Just the ball scene, in which the handsome, quixotic, charming Max Vanderhorn had seduced Queen Margot in full view of a thousand guests with just his voice and his thumbs had sent the temperature in the theater up at least fifteen degrees.

*Man of the Hour*. Never in her life had Dulcy wished for anything but what she had. Suddenly she wanted to smile like that queen had in Max's arms. Suddenly she wanted to dance so fast the room spun around her. She wanted to find herself in a fantasy in which she was the sole sight in a handsome man's eyes.

Even so, she turned back on her disheveled, scruffy boss and her plump, pretty cousin and her much-too-grown-up daughter, and she gave them the final word.

"Find me one person in a tiara and sash tonight who isn't finalist for Miss Corn Crop," she challenged them both, "and I'll get up on the bandstand and sing the *Man of the Hour* theme a cappella. Now let's get going before I change my mind altogether."

It was another beautiful night. Above the half-finished barn, the sky arced away in deepening peacock like a silk blanket frayed at the edges by crimson. The breeze tugged at skirts and ruffled hair, and the lights strung along the beams gleamed gently on friendly faces. After a hard week of branding and a long day of carpentry, the neighborhood had gathered to relax, and relax they did. Children scampered around, preteens clustered in stiff groups to eye the groups of the other sex. Parents shared gossip and pocket flasks. In the corner the band warmed up, and at the back a table laden with potluck offerings attracted a steady line.

Dulcy felt as if she belonged with those teens, the gangly, uncertain ones who were still too long-limbed or acne afflicted. The ones not sure of their graces, their attraction or their place. She had never felt this way at thirteen. Amazing she should now.

"You're saving some of the slow dances for me, aren't you?" Noah asked in her ear.

Dulcy fought the inevitable fall of shivers his close voice incited. "I'm not much of a dancer, Noah."

His chuckle should have been included in the encyclopedia of sin. "I doubt that."

And then, without another word, he was gone. Weaving his way through the crowd that greeted him with the ease of a longtime neighbor, a backslap here and there from the ones who hadn't had a chance to laugh over his introduction to town down at the Lone Star, a smile and a simper from the women who'd already heard on the grapevine how attractive their new neighbor was.

Well, Noah was. Attractive and charming and more. Dulcy, as usual, took her place along the chairs by the food and punch where she could catch up on the news and ignore the people who would ignore her. She kissed Miss Retta on the cheek and laughed with Vera and a couple of the mothers from school as if nothing were unusual, as if every one of them didn't notice that no matter how hard she tried to the contrary, there was something very different about her tonight. She gossiped and visited, and knew every second of the time just where Noah was in the big, open building.

"He's quite a lovely young man," Miss Retta offered coyly from where she sat on a folding chair like a deb at her first ball. "And such a gentleman in the face of your rather formidable aunt."

"Yes," Dulcy answered automatically. "Wasn't he?"

He should have said something to her by now. She knew about the phone call Ethan had made. Knew just what Noah had found if he'd booted up the computer, which he had. She'd heard him.

And yet, he hadn't said a word.

Why?

Dulcy had been trying so hard in the small hours of the night when he'd been asleep to find the problem. She'd sent Noah out with the men to ride fences and learn the land, and she'd gone off in different directions with Hank to see what they could find that might explain their losses.

She hadn't made any headway. Noah had to know that.

And yet, he hadn't asked.

"Where'd he say he was from?" somebody else asked, all eyes tracking Noah like the royal box checking out serves at Wimbledon.

"Philadelphia."

"But he has a Texan accent, doesn't he?"

"Uh-huh. He grew up there." At least, he'd intimated he had. Dulcy didn't really know for sure.

. She really didn't know anything for sure about him, except what he'd told her, which was nothing. Except what she'd found out, which wasn't important. She didn't know where he'd been raised, who his family was, what had shaped him and led him here.

She didn't know what had given birth to that longing she'd surprised in his eyes when he'd looked on the land, or the loneliness she suspected in the fact that in the time he'd been there not one person from his other life had contacted him.

In fact, the only other person she knew about in that other world was the ubiquitous Ethan, the one who always answered when she called, who always fielded the questions and put together the deals. Ethan, who sounded a lot like Noah, but without the accent.

Without the underlying intensity.

Ethan, who seemed to be Noah's filter between the real world and this one.

Dulcy wondered why. She watched him move so easily among the people of this valley, as if he'd belonged here his whole life, and wondered what it was he kept from here.

What he kept from his other life.

He walked right up to where she was standing, his eyes alight, a cup of punch in his hand. Dulcy almost stopped breathing on the spot.

"Ladies," he said, acknowledging the little cluster of women who all smiled back. "How are you all tonight?"

"You've been holding back on us," Miss Retta accused.

Noah let an eyebrow slide north as he bent toward her, every inch the devoted gentleman. "How's that, Miss Retta?"

She waggled a finger at him. "Just where did a businessman from Philadelphia learn so much about building barns?"

He laughed. "Same place I learned how to ride a horse. My uncle's ranch in Texas. I learned all my practical skills there."

"Did you learn how to dance?" she asked, as if announcing the next song. Behind them the band swung into a lively two-step.

Noah's face fell. "My uncle was a heck of a horseman," he apologized. "But not much on his feet. Probably too late now to learn, I'm afraid."

Miss Retta straightened to the full extent of her genteel dignity. "It's never too late to learn, young man. Not to learn properly, at any rate."

Noah's smile almost melted the plastic cup in Dulcy's hand. "Miss Retta," he countered. "Is that a challenge I hear?"

Miss Retta climbed to her not very considerable feet. "It seems it is, Mr. Campbell. Are you up to it?"

When Noah reached out to take Miss Retta's hand, every eye within twenty feet misted over. When he let her lead him out onto the floor, everyone watched. Even Dulcy. Especially Dulcy.

Miss Retta hadn't joined in one of these dances as long as Dulcy had known her. No man in town had asked her. No one had thought....

Noah had.

He bent over her now, his eyes alight, his smile as true as sunlight, his concentration on Miss Retta as if she were Scarlet O'Hara. Other people danced out on that floor. Even their attention was on the mismatched couple, and smiles grew like wildflowers before Noah Campbell's sun.

Dulcy shouldn't have been impressed. She shouldn't have been enchanted. She shouldn't have forgotten for one moment just how foolish it would be to fall in love with her boss.

"Oh, my God," Sally breathed again, her voice hushed with true awe. "It is *Man of the Hour*."

Oh, my God. Dulcy couldn't have put it any better.

Noah danced with the little woman for three dances, the two-step and two slower waltzes. He stumbled a little and laughed and tried again until he looked almost as comfortable as his teacher. And then he brought her from the dance floor flushed and smiling in a way Dulcy had never seen in her life. He gave that lovely, well-known little woman something none of her friends had thought to give her, and Dulcy couldn't manage the words that would thank him.

"And now," he said, turning her way after making sure Miss Retta had her chair and her punch, "I think it's time I tried this dancing stuff out on you."

Dulcy almost turned around to see who was standing in back of her. "What?"

His smile grew to near-wicked proportions. "Well, now that I've learned how to do it, I thought I should put it to use. Before I forget it again, ya know?"

"Oh, I don't . . ."

Someone gave her a push that landed her almost smack in Noah's arms.

"Sure you do," he said for her and took hold of her hand.

It had been so long since Dulcy had allowed herself fantasies that she had no preparation for what she faced out on that dance floor. She hadn't dreamed into the night of the seductive feel of a man matching her step for step across a wood plank floor. She hadn't imagined the rasp of his work-roughened fingers along her back. She hadn't allowed herself to ever imagine the heady warmth of his gaze on her alone as the floor and the people and the lights whirled by.

The band consisted of a couple of fiddles, a guitar and a mandolin. The music was as homespun as local humor. Even though she hadn't done it much, Dulcy had danced in barns before, finished and not. Sally's husband Bart had made it a point to get her to join in.

She'd never in her life spent five minutes like this.

Noah wrapped his fingers through hers and slipped his other hand around her waist. He focused his eyes on her as if she were his point of balance, and he led her around the room with unerring ease. He smiled at her as if what they were doing was a stupid joke everyone else could join in on, and yet, beneath that smile, Noah was letting her know something more. Something dangerous. Something heady and wonderful and wild.

Dulcy could swear she could almost hear him, like a humming along the edges of her fingers, a whisper in her ear she should catch if she turned her head quickly enough. A throb just beneath the sound of the music that no one else could pick up. She felt her skirt skim her bare legs and the air brush her calves. She felt Noah's thighs slide alongside hers as they moved. She saw the lights glitter in his eyes and smelled the tang of his after-shave. She felt as if she were melting and freezing at the same time. As if she were struck dumb and yet wanted to tell him everything.

She felt as if once he set her back among her friends she'd keep spinning.

"This is stupid" was all she could say, unable to pull her gaze from his. Mesmerized by perfectly ordinary gray eyes.

"I know," he answered, his voice a caress, his eyes dancing with humor.

"Then you know we shouldn't be doing it."

"Why? Because I'm your boss, or because you're enjoying it?"

Dulcy couldn't manage a lie simply because it was wise. "Both," she challenged and made him laugh.

"Me, too. But then, I thought you didn't care what people thought."

"I don't...I do." She shook her head in frustration, only to be startled by the unfamiliar shudder of hair against her shoulders. "I don't need them to get the wrong idea about why I got this job...look at me when you answer."

"I am looking at you," he insisted lazily. "I've been thinking about looking at you on the dance floor since Sally first told me about the dance. I have to admit, I'm not disappointed."

At least she could scowl at that. "Please, don't," she objected dryly. "The flattery will go to my silly head."

His gaze met hers again, and she almost stumbled. "Your hair is magnificent. Has anybody told you that?"

"Yes. And when I listened to him, I went from English class to prenatal class. You lied to Miss Retta."

Spinning, surging, sweeping past all the people in her life as if they didn't matter anymore. As if their place had been superseded. Still Dulcy couldn't take her eyes from Noah's.

"I never lie," he protested.

"If you've never danced," she retorted, "I've never changed diapers."

His smile was bright and happy. "Oh, that. It wasn't a lie. It was a . . . pick-up line."

Dulcy couldn't believe it. She laughed. It felt wonderful. *She* felt wonderful, as bubbly and light and graceful as she'd ever wanted to in those distant days when she'd only meant to outrage her very stiff parents.

"Thank you," she said, anyway. "You made a very nice lady happy."

"What about you?" he asked, leaning a little closer. "Am I making you happy?"

The music ended before Dulcy could answer. Before she could get her heart to slow enough for her to catch a decent breath.

"There's something you should know," she said, standing there stock-still in the middle of the dance floor as other couples trickled by toward food and drink.

Noah couldn't seem to look serious. "What's that?"

"I haven't been honest about the ranch."

Dulcy wasn't sure what she expected. She still wasn't sure why, after all the work to the contrary, she'd said it, except that it was the surest way she could think of to put some distance between her and her new boss.

She wasn't prepared for Noah to grin.

"Finally," he said, taking her hand and turning her toward the punch. "I thought you'd never say anything."

That brought Dulcy to a full stop. In the corner the band swung into the "Orange Blossom Special," and a few of the hardier kids came out to celebrate. Dulcy and Noah stood faced off.

"What does that mean?" she demanded.

"It means," he said gently, "that when we get home from the dance we'll start to work it out."

"You knew."

He nodded. "And you knew I knew. Why didn't you say something?"

"Why didn't *you?*"

His chuckle was indecent. "Is this what marriage is like?" he asked, and then tugged her off the dance floor before they got run over.

"You should have fired me," she insisted.

They got as far as the line of chairs. "Probably," he acknowledged, then faced her with as much sincerity as was in him on a night like this. "But only because you wouldn't trust me to understand."

"Understand what?" she retorted. "That you're missing cattle and the spread sheet doesn't add up?"

"Ethan and I already figured out what was wrong with the spread sheet. If you'd come to me about it, we could have had this conversation before we got all dressed up. Now, let's enjoy ourselves and leave the problems at the ranch until later."

There were a lot of things Dulcy could have said. All she could manage was to ask, "You figured it out?"

Noah's smile this time was simple. "Yes. Now then, I came here to dance, and I'm going to do it. I'm going to do it with you, because I find that I can't keep my hands off you, no matter who the boss is and who's here to see him act like an idiot." With that, he lifted a hand to run his thumb along the curve of her jaw. "I have the most horrible feeling, Ms. McCann, that the entire community is going to see me make cow eyes at you tonight. And even confessing to lying to me about the ranch isn't going to dissuade me."

It wasn't Noah who looked like an idiot. When he strolled over to get drink refills, Dulcy found herself left behind gaping like a landed fish.

Cow eyes? Who was he kidding? What did he mean?

He couldn't possibly mean what Dulcy was afraid he meant. He couldn't mean that he was still humming like an electrified wire just from having held her. He couldn't mean that the air seemed to empty out the farther away she got. He couldn't mean that he couldn't seem to get enough of the sight of perfectly ordinary eyes.

Oh, God, she thought in absolute despair. Of all the places to realize that she was falling in love, it had to be in the middle of a dance where every living person in the valley could watch.

It had to be with the man who'd insisted on keeping her on against everyone's better judgment.

It had to be a man who kept his own secrets even better than he kept his business—and that should have made Dulcy angriest of all.

"Guess some of us just don't have the same advantages as others," she heard under somebody's breath.

"Yeah. All Hank has to offer is twenty-five years' experience."

"Not to mention poor Josh. I still say it's a sin that he didn't get what was due him."

It was nothing new under the sun. Dulcy had heard the accusations since she'd returned to the valley and taken over the ranch for Aunt Cordelia. Since she'd brought her little girl along as if the entire area didn't know just what that particular story was.

It hurt this time. Their accusations felt so very unfair. Not because their attitudes had changed. But because hers had. Because she'd worked so hard for what she had and she could see its worth dimming in the face of an attraction she hadn't anticipated.

An attraction she'd never wanted.

An attraction that had long since become something far more.

"Hey, Dulce, wanna dance?"

Dulcy turned around to see the sweet, homely face of Bart Bixby beaming on her. Sent, no doubt, by Sally to counter some of the petty spite she'd probably overheard.

It was the last thing she felt like doing in the world right then, but Dulcy smiled. "Thank you, sweetie. I'd love to."

And so Bart took her out on the floor and stepped on her toes, and Dulcy thought about what she'd missed all these years out on a dance floor with only her cousin to keep her company. And when she walked off the dance floor, she kept on going until she found herself alone at the edge of the Tilton's meadow where nobody could judge her.

"I didn't think you were a coward," he said when he found her.

Dulcy didn't turn away from where she was considering the darkness beyond the lights and music of the dance. "I've been called lots of names in my life," she said evenly without turning to face him. "That's probably the only one not on the list."

"Then why didn't you stay there and face them?"

That got her to turn around. She couldn't see Noah's eyes. They were in shadows. His entire face was shadowed, as if Dulcy had just imagined him out of the cloth of her loneliness. The loneliness she hadn't even admitted until he'd stumbled into her house.

His house.

Her life.

"Did you live in one place your whole life?" she asked.

"No. I told you that."

"You haven't told me anything. How many places did you live?"

When he answered, his voice was a little smaller. "What's that got to do with it?"

"Everything."

Dulcy waited. Noah stood there before her, hands in jacket pockets, head up as if preparing to defend himself. A position she knew all too well. One she hadn't expected to see on him.

"So we traveled around a little. What's that got to do with it?"

"Everything. You could reinvent yourself every time you went someplace new," she challenged. "I can't. There's no crowd to hide in, no brand new start where nobody knows what's gone before. I have to live with every mistake I've ever made. Every blunder, every humiliation... No matter how well I do—and I've done *damn* well, Noah—what I did when I was sixteen always comes back to haunt me."

"Meaning?"

"Meaning that I worked too damn hard to end right back in that pool of water. I spent the last eight years making sure that

the people in this valley would understand that I didn't live up
to all of their worst expectations."

"And being attracted to me would ruin that?"

"Being attracted to you would set me back so far that getting pregnant at sixteen wouldn't even be a problem anymore."

"Then why stay?"

"Because, damn it, I should be able to. It's my home. My
family's here. No one should be able to run me off."

"But should they be able to make you miserable?"

Now her chin came up. "They don't."

"They do." Noah stepped up to her, so close he blotted out
most of the light, so close she could smell the soft whisper of
soap on him. So close she fought just to breathe. "They made
you into a nun, Dulcy." He lifted a hand, brought it to her hair,
let his fingers explore. "A sexless, cloistered, careful nun. Except that your habit is work boots and jeans instead of a veil."

"They didn't…" Dulcy couldn't think. Noah's fingers were
inciting a shower of sparks along her neck. She'd never had a
man's hands in her hair. Not like this. Not as if he couldn't keep
his hands away, as if he were ingesting life from her through his
fingertips.

"You don't even go to movies," he said, his face so close now
she could see his eyes. His ghostly eyes. His ordinary, moon-
swept eyes. "No dreams, no fantasies, no fun. The only person you really let in is Hannah, and that's not enough, Dulcy.
It's just not enough."

Dulcy tried so hard to think. To object. "Sweaty palms isn't
reason enough to throw away everything I've achieved, either," she finally managed to say, backing away against the
fence. "I know. I've done it once, remember?"

His hand was still wound in her hair. He lifted the other to
her chin, to lift her face to his. To force her to face the sky, as
if she had a right to it.

"If this were just sweaty palms, Dulcy, I'd be the first one in
a cold shower." He chuckled, a rasp of surprise. "After all, I
came here figuring I wouldn't look at another woman as long
as I lived."

Dulcy laughed back, but the sound was high and much too
breathless to be sarcastic. "Didn't do a very good job of it."

"I know." He shook his head slowly, moved closer. "I know. Tell me what I should do."

He didn't wait for an answer. Before Dulcy could draw breath, he caught her mouth in a kiss. A real kiss, the kind that young girls dream of, soft and questing and sweet. His hands slipping along her throat and urging her closer.

Dulcy tried so hard to fight what was already a losing battle. "You shouldn't play stupid . . . ah, games . . ."

His mouth was so hot, so nourishing and alive. His hands were so strong, big enough to carry, gentle enough to share. "I didn't mean . . ."

"I can't . . ." Dulcy forgot what it was she couldn't.

She rose on her toes, lifted her own hands. Wrapped herself up in the thick luxury of Noah's hair and took her own taste of him. Sweet punch and sharp whiskey and dark silk. Mastery and submission. Dulcy felt the rumble of a groan against her fingertips and shuddered with its power.

In the distance she heard the band swing into another song, something slow and sad, one of the ballads brought west about love lost and lonely wandering. Dulcy heard the minor notes wind through the summer night, felt them take wing in her as if their slow, thick cadence set the dance of Noah's fingers. As if their pain echoed in the lonely places Dulcy had never expected in him.

Need.

Want.

Hunger.

Dulcy tasted them all on him, offered them back. Fed her own need with the rasp of his beard against her hands, the almost clumsy impatience of his hands against her waist, her back, her arms. She lifted against him, opened to him, begged him open in return. She held on, not because he was strong. Because he smiled. Because he courted old women and laughed with little girls.

She encouraged, because his touch brought her back to life, even though it hurt.

It hurt.

"Why me?" she asked, sounding so much like the sad song other people danced to.

Noah pulled her close, bent his head over hers. Held on tight, as if afraid of losing what he'd found.

"Dulcy..."

"I mean it..." She had to drag in her breath, like yanking on a hand brake. She had to understand, because her body was already way ahead of sense here, and she knew better. "It's only been a week, Noah. I don't understand it."

His laugh was sharp and surprised. "Don't look for explanations from me. Ethan was trying to tell me about profit and loss, and all I could seem to talk to him about was what your hair looked like."

"I've tried so hard to be sensible."

"I don't think sense is involved here."

"I *know* it isn't." Tears now, welling in the back of her throat like hot tar. Stupid, useless things that only meant she was much more confused than she'd thought. That this had gotten far too far out of hand. "I have to get back to Hannah."

"Not yet," he begged. Begged, as if Dulcy were that important. "Please."

She squeezed her eyes shut and pretended. Just for a moment. It was something she hadn't done for so long, she knew she got it wrong, because what she saw was her and Noah and Hannah. On the ranch. Happy. Whole. She saw something she'd never allowed before, not once in all these years.

She saw a family, and that stopped her cold.

"I can't, Noah," she said, not moving.

"You can do anything, Dulcy."

He sounded afraid.

Afraid. Dulcy thought she was the only one who was afraid. So unnerved that her heart was hammering and her skin tingled in a thousand places.

Somehow she'd been struck by lightning, and she was reeling.

"You have to tell me about the books," she insisted even as he tilted her head back again.

"Later."

"I have to find those lost cattle."

He kissed her again, nipping at her lower lip and letting his hand stray from the corner of her jaw. "In the morning."

She sobbed with the effort to stand up. To stand still. To not take hold of his hand and just place it over her breast. To place it lower, where her body was starting to revolt against all that control she'd exerted over it along the years.

"No, Noah," she begged, knowing damn well he heard what she was really saying.

His hand found the tender skin over her heart. His fingers, so calloused and warm slipped beneath her camisole, and she let him. She felt her head fall back to give him better access, felt her thick, unruly hair brush across her back.

"Yes, Dulcy."

He dipped to taste her throat with his tongue and her nipple with his thumb, and Dulcy let him. She begged him. She wanted him.

"Please..."

Please what? Please stop? Please don't? She didn't know anymore.

"Please..."

His hands, on her skin, tracing her lips, her eyes, tangled in her hair. His mouth, warming her, chilling her, nourishing her. Her body, shimmering with sudden, stunning need.

And then, suddenly, he stopped.

Dulcy was still dragging in a breath, wondering what had happened to those wonderful hands. Already Noah was four paces away, and his eyes were in the shadow again.

"What's wrong?" she asked.

"What's wrong?" he retorted, his voice suddenly sharp and certain. "What's wrong is that I can't get a straight answer from you about what's going on."

# Nine

Noah felt as if he'd just been thrown in a blender on puree.

"What?" Dulcy whispered, her body rigid, her eyes huge.

He opened his mouth to further the lie. To protect her.

"Don't get all businesslike on my account," he heard someone say behind him. "It's just me."

Sally.

Somehow he'd heard her, some sixth sense from his other life that kept on alert for camera-carrying paparazzi even as his body spiraled out of control. It had been a very close thing, though.

"Sure nice to see you, Sally," Noah lazily greeted Dulcy's cousin as he surreptitiously pulled Dulcy's vest back into place. As he sucked in some settling air and tried hard to keep his hands from shaking as badly as the rest of him.

"Better me than Mary Murphy," Sally retorted as she reached them. "She's in there pumping Josh for all the dirt on the ranch. I think your dancing exhibition inspired her."

Dulcy groaned. "Oh, great. And I just got her to stop calling me a strumpet from the last time."

"The last time?" Sally echoed.

"Strumpet?" Noah laughed. "Them's mighty strong words."

"I was mighty single when I had that baby," Dulcy reminded him, her hand on his arm, her fingers tight in a silent thanks. "Aunt Mary is nothing if not scrupulously honest."

"And law abiding," Sally added.

"And shrewish," Noah chimed in.

Sally made it a point to turn back to consider the action behind them. "The perfect relative. Glad she's not mine."

"She's Bart's," Dulcy reminded her.

"Remind me to stop by for a scorecard before I leave," Noah said.

"Bart's over by the Tilton's house, Dulcy," Sally said. "You'll walk back in with him. Noah and I'll just wait here for a minute."

"We're big kids," Dulcy began to protest.

"Why don't I go back with Bart?" Noah asked. "It might look better."

"You kidding?" Sally retorted, seriously outraged. "And deprive me of the only good rumor ever started about me in this godforsaken place?"

Noah scowled, more grateful than he knew how to say for the time she'd given them both. "Bart isn't appreciably bigger than I am, is he?"

Sally's grin was pure mischief. "He could beat you like a rented mule, if he wanted. Fortunately, he won't. Bart respects nothing as much as a well-cooked meal. And I cook the best meals in three states. Now, go on, Dulcy, before the other half of the dance knows what you two have been up to."

It took Dulcy a second to relent. "This isn't necessary, ya know."

Sally grinned. "I know. It is . . . judicious, though. At least for now."

Without another word, Dulcy turned back for the dance, and Noah watched her go. The lights caught faint ruby highlights in her hair and evaporated the solid outline of her skirt so he could watch the shadows of her legs as she walked. He could remember the feel of her against his hands. The terrible sense that this, finally, was what he needed. What he wanted. What he could never have.

"You can't get a better manager than Dulcy," Sally said evenly.

Noah looked over to see Sally watching the same thing he was. "I know."

She nodded, arms akimbo, set in a position of judgment. "Puts the Ponderosa to shame."

Ponderosa as in "Bonanza," Noah imagined. "I know that."

"No matter what you think's going on."

"What do I think is going on?"

She looked at him, and he saw very sharp blue eyes. "You tell me."

"Your job is safe, Sally," he said, "if that's what you mean."

"That's nice. Did I tell you I only work at that ranch because Dulcy's there?"

"What do you think I'm going to do?" he countered. "Sell the thing to Jack Palance and throw Dulcy out?"

"I think you're going to be here for about four more weeks and then disappear again."

Noah couldn't think of a thing to say to that.

Sally faced him, and he saw what kind of effort it took.

"I'm being totally out of line," she informed him. "But I don't care much. I've been with Dulcy every step of the way since the day she told her father she was pregnant. I know what she's accomplished. I know what she's overcome. I know that I told her I thought you could be good for her. I want to make sure I was right."

Noah let out a laugh that sounded suspiciously like a sigh. "You this involved with all your cousins?"

Sally looked back toward the dance, where the men had begun to cluster outside to share drinks and fishing stories. "Did Dulcy tell you what happened the day she graduated from college?"

Noah didn't answer. He knew he didn't have to.

"Her mom and dad are big education people. The other kids have degrees, which the Rev and Missus paid for. Nice jobs, careers, you know. Anyway, when the ceremony was over, Dulcy didn't even take off her cap and gown. She piled Hannah in the car and headed on over to Billings to let them know that it might have taken her six years, but she'd done it. She'd worked two part-time jobs and not slept for weeks on end and single-handedly raised a beautiful little girl, but she'd gotten her bachelor's. She'd done what they'd wanted."

"They didn't come to the graduation?"

"God, no. She never expected that. She did think they'd at least see her at the house, though." Sally sighed. "She got to the house and found it empty. The neighbors told her that her parents had left for a trip two days earlier. Deliberately. They were afraid she'd come see them, and they figured being gone was the best way to avoid an unpleasant situation."

"Unpleasant?"

Sally's smile was dark. "Wouldn't it be nice if we were all altruistic people? Even after getting pregnant, Dulcy might have been allowed back in the fold if she'd seen the light and let Hannah be adopted out, so the whole thing could be swept under the rug. That was her father's price for letting her come home and have her education paid for."

Noah's gaze strayed toward the dance, where he could see a lithe figure with flaming hair strolling arm in arm with a bear of a man. He thought about not being able to go home and what that cost.

"She had you," he said to Sally.

"Me?" Sally laughed. "I knew all along that her parents weren't going to be there. I didn't have the guts to tell her. I still don't." Sally turned on him, pinned him in his place. "This last couple of years Dulcy has been the happiest I've ever seen her. She has Hannah, she has work she loves, she has a place she's beginning to call home. I just don't think it would be fair for her to start believing in something that isn't going to be there when she rings the doorbell, ya know?"

He knew.

"I don't care who you are," Sally challenged. "I can't let you hurt her."

Noah dragged a hand through his hair. "You can't think I can promise not to hurt her, can you?"

"You can give me a promise of good faith."

"Sally, I'm as surprised by this as Dulcy is. Believe me."

"I believe you. It doesn't mean I trust you."

Noah couldn't help it. Even still feeling as if he'd been caught in chopper blades, he had to grin at her. "It's too bad you're busy here," he admitted. "I could use you in my other life."

"You couldn't afford me."

He wanted to walk around, to kick the dirt a little, consider the moon. He ended up standing stock-still, facing this formidable woman over an issue he didn't understand himself. "All I can promise is this. I don't make commitments lightly. I've made one to the ranch, and that's that. Nobody's pushing me off, turning me away or buying me out. I've wanted this too long. As for Dulcy, I've never felt this way about anyone in my life—"

"Even the woman you were mourning at the Last Chance the first night?"

He smiled. "Even her. I know some of what Dulcy has been facing, and the last thing I want to do is put her through more. Trust me, if I could figure a way past all that, I'd do it. But Sally..." He lifted his hands, ineffective gestures of how overwhelmed he was. "I couldn't stop now if you held a gun to my head."

She didn't appear to be moved. "Is that your heart speaking, or your fly?"

He laughed, shaking his head. "Every inch of me. So, if you want to have Bart beat me stupid, go right ahead. It isn't going to change anything."

Sally glared at him a moment longer, divining his intentions in the dark, he guessed. Then as suddenly as she'd pounced on him, she retreated. Grinned. Grabbed his arm and turned him for the dance.

"*Gone with the Wind,*" she said happily.

"Huh?"

Sally patted his arm and laughed. "Never mind."

"So it was deliberate sabotage," Dulcy concluded the next afternoon as she leaned over Noah's shoulder to squint at the computer screen in her office.

"That's what we figured," Noah assured her. "Ethan had uploaded all the information on the ranch the week we closed. When he went to update the information, it was inexplicably changed. We spent all of one night working on numbers and got nowhere.''

"I know the feeling.''

"Ethan was the one who finally cracked it. Nothing more than computer games from one modem to another.''

Dulcy straightened and rubbed her eyes. "I've been killing myself over this stuff. It looked so damning.''

"I know. I guess that was the idea. Especially since the cattle were missing.''

She sighed and sat back, exhausted. It was what happened when a person didn't get any sleep and then spent the day wrestling large animals and evenings wrestling small computers. It especially happened when that person couldn't keep her mind on the job at hand.

"I'm sorry, Noah.''

"For what?'' he countered, looking over the tops of his wire-rim glasses at her. "Not believing I'd be smart enough to figure out that you were the last person on earth who'd want to cheat me?''

She considered him for a moment. With those glasses he looked like an overeducated hobo. His beard was getting really scruffy and his face wind chapped and sunburned. His eyes looked so pale against his face. His hair was getting shaggy and sun-streaked. Dulcy had never seen a more magnetic man in her life.

"I hadn't even met you when you were poured into this house the first day,'' she reminded him. "How the heck was I supposed to know what you were going to think?''

He shrugged and went back to the numbers. "Point taken. Now you know, though. You should know enough to trust me.''

"Just like you trust me.''

"Exactly.''

"Which was why you let me in on the fact that you knew about the books not balancing right away.''

That got his full attention. "Ah,'' he said with a nod. "Yes. There is that.''

"We don't have time to play games here, Noah,'' she reminded him.

"You wanted me to yell at you right away.''

"Would you have waited for Hank to tell you?"

For a very long moment, Noah just watched her. Just tapped his fingers against the edge of the desk as if counting cadence with his thoughts.

"No," he finally said, climbing to his feet. "I guess I wouldn't."

Dulcy nodded. "I don't deserve any less."

For a minute he just stood there before her, eyes hooded, hands jammed into pockets, attention on her like a laser. Then he simply shook his head. "You're right," he said. "I'm sorry. It isn't that you don't deserve it. It's that . . . well, things have become more complicated."

Dulcy tried so hard to throw off a nod, as if it were all as easy as a snappy comeback. "*Complicated* is a good word."

He grinned, relief evidently warring with frustration. "I wish I could say I was making sense. But everything's changed, and I don't know what to do about it. And truth be told, except for Ethan, I haven't had many people I've been able to trust lately."

Dulcy wondered if he heard the edge to his voice when he said that. "Just you and Ethan against the world, huh?"

He shrugged. "Always been that way."

She nodded, her gaze slipping down to the tips of her boots, suddenly too close to Noah for comfort. Too near the truth to back away. "I get the feeling you don't like to rely on people much. You don't have friends, people you can really open up to, tell the truth to and chance all that horrible exposure that so terrifies us all."

"Something you're conversant with, I guess."

"Used to be," she admitted, facing him again. Forcing herself to confront the need she recognized in another person's eyes. "But that's what home's for. I do have friends and family here I can count on."

Somehow that seemed to steal some of the light from Noah's eyes. He nodded as if hearing a myth. "Yeah, well. I never—" He struggled, stopped. Lifted his head as if the weight of what he needed to tell her grew too great. "Except for Ethan, I didn't really have roots. No place like this I could rely on."

"Even your uncle's ranch?"

Another small smile, a very careful lifting of the shoulders.
"I guess that's as close as it got."

Such a simple admission. Carried on rigid shoulders and
impossibly correct posture. Dulcy thought prisoners of war
must look just like this when offering up secrets they had carried like hot stones.

This man who had everything, who mesmerized with his
voice and his eyes, who had the fortune to buy a prosperous
ranch for cash, who commanded respect and admiration. This
man was alone.

This man was lonely.

God, Dulcy wanted to hold him. To just whisper that she was
there now. That it would be all right if he could just trust her.

But trust was still a long way off. Understanding, commit-
ment, sense. Right now all she had was a raw ache in the pit of
her stomach from wanting more from him even when she knew
how really stupid an idea that was.

"Then I guess," she said, her own voice tight as her posture, "that you'll just have to make this your home."

He looked up, a wealth of memory in his eyes, echoes of
emotions and passions that seemed too great for the daylight
and this prim little room with its rosebud wallpaper. Dulcy
stood still before him, not knowing what else to do, not knowing how to answer a challenge as great as his.

Wanting to.

"What now?" Noah asked, and Dulcy knew he wasn't asking about work. He wasn't asking about business or cattle or
the life in the house around them.

Downstairs the phone rang. Dulcy ignored it. Sally'd let her
know if it was something important.

"Now," she said carefully, her voice unforgivably tight as she
deliberately misunderstood him, "we try and figure out who's
stealing your cattle so you don't lose everything you have on a
ranch you've wanted all your life."

"Mom!" Hannah yelled up the stairs. "Uncle Mike's on the
phone! Says it's important!"

Dulcy apologized with her eyes. With the helpless lifting of
her hands that excused her escape to business. And before
Noah could see through the obvious retreat, she fled.

* * *

"Sorry, honey," her Uncle Mike said, his voice loud and efficient. "Couple of my hands just got back from town. Told me when they went over Wilson Creek Road they spotted some fencing down. You've got loose cattle."

"Thanks, Uncle Mike."

Dulcy was already in the process of grabbing hat, gloves and keys when Noah caught up with her.

"Dulcy?"

"The business discussions are going to have to wait, Noah. We have some cattle loose and some fences down. Wanna come along?"

He answered by grabbing his own gear.

Dulcy took a second to give Hannah a hug and kiss. "Want to ride up with us?"

Hannah scowled. "Can I stay here and listen to the music?"

Dulcy scowled right back, an old game. God had obviously given her somebody else's child, someone with culture and artistic brilliance. Someone who adored cattle, but only from upwind.

"Oh, I suppose if you must. But that means lots of practicing while I'm gone so you can support me in my old age."

"Mo-o-om." A flash of a grin, like a shaft of sunlight through troubled clouds. It was worth everything Dulcy had survived. Would survive.

"Try the Cranberries CD," Noah suggested as he followed. He only waited until the screen door slammed behind them to turn his attention back to Dulcy. "We're going to have to talk. You know that."

"Later," she said as easily as she knew how. "Right now we have to get those cattle before an eighteen-wheeler makes steak *tartare* out of 'em."

Since they found Hank right away, that was the last of that.

Technically the delaying tactic worked. Gathering a couple of trucks, a couple of dogs and a couple of horses, Dulcy set out with Hank, Noah and Paco to get the cattle back into pasture and the fences mended. It took the rest of the afternoon, and much of the early evening hours. By the time they got back, they were all dirty, tired and crabby. And they were supposed to begin moving the cattle up to summer pasture the next day, which would take at least two days. Dulcy grabbed a sandwich for dinner and a shower afterward, taking an inordinate time washing her hair and ignoring the music skittering from the living room where Hannah and Noah were inventing a Hootie duet for violin and piano. She made a final check on the animals and said good-night to Hank, then spent another hour in reading *Lord of the Rings* to Hannah, who'd heard it all before but didn't in the least mind playing the part of Gollim again.

When Dulcy came downstairs again, the house was quiet. Her tennis shoes shushed against the hardwood floor, and her damp hair caught the currents from the open front door. She knew she had no business heading for the porch. Noah would be there. She went anyway.

"How would you like to do me a favor?" Noah asked without looking around.

"How'd you know I was here?" she asked through the screen door.

"I always know where you are," he said, still leaning against the porch railing, his T-shirt gleaming softly in the night, his jeans old and battered and sagging a little across the butt. "Will you do me a favor?"

"What?"

"Redecorate the house."

That got Dulcy to push open the door and walk out on the porch. "Redecorate it? Just like that?"

When he looked over, she faltered to a halt. "Just like that."

"What do you want?"

Noah shrugged. "I stink at that kind of thing. I just know I don't want green and gold brocade and pressboard entertainment systems." Like the one presently in the living room that had belonged to her frugal, tasteless aunt. "Leave the dining room be, though. I like that old table."

"You want antiques then?"

"Functional ones, I guess. Something I'd be comfortable on."

"Okay."

His one eyebrow lifted. "Just like that?"

Dulcy shrugged, knowing perfectly well she couldn't betray any of the emotions warring in her. "Your house."

"No," he objected, a finger up. "My *home*."

Dulcy didn't know how to answer. She didn't know what to do with the sudden intensity in his eyes, or the ambivalence his words engendered in her.

"Okay," she said with a stiff nod. "Sure."

"Great. Then it's settled."

Noah turned back to his consideration of the night, and Dulcy turned to go back in the house.

"There's something you need to know," he said.

Dulcy stopped, suddenly, inexplicably afraid. "No I don't."

"Your cousin Sally chewed me out last night."

Dulcy wanted to laugh. Somehow, she couldn't. "Great. That's just what I need."

Noah didn't seem to hear her. Dulcy turned to see him considering the stars, and she wanted to reach out to him. She wanted to touch him, to make sure he was real. She stood perfectly still instead.

Noah didn't turn around. "For a woman who lives on movies," he said, "she seems awfully unconvinced that a person can fall in love in a week."

Dulcy couldn't breathe. She could hardly stand up. She couldn't look away, even though she knew he'd catch her lying. "Well, then," she managed to say. "She and I have something in common."

Noah should have been more disconcerted. He should have at least been as breathless as Dulcy was. "No surprise, I guess," he said evenly, finally turning to her. "Until I came here, I would have agreed with you."

Don't, Dulcy wanted to beg. Don't push so hard. Don't bring up things we have no business talking about. Wishing for. Expecting.

Don't think I can offer everything without getting anything in return.

Her heart was hammering as if she'd run a long way. Her chest felt on fire. She was most terrified of hearing what she wanted to hear the most, of finding what she saw in his eyes.

Dulcy didn't realize she was going to run until she did it, spinning for the steps and heading straight across the lawn.

Going nowhere except away from Noah and the moment they'd been heading toward since he'd first opened his eyes.

She heard the thud of his feet on the steps, felt him closing in like a storm front.

"We have to at least talk," he demanded, catching hold of her out under the huge old oak.

Dulcy shuddered to a halt. "No we don't," she all but begged. "We can act like professionals and run this ranch until you go back to the real world."

"I'm happy here, Dulcy," Noah said simply, his posture as intent as his words. "Can't you let me be happy with you?"

She turned on him then, not sure what she wanted. Not sure what she dreaded or believed. "And that's all there is to it? Us being happy here on the ranch for six weeks at a time?"

Dulcy saw him hesitate, straighten. "No. I guess not."

"Contrary to what my past might suggest," she said. "I'm not a person given to flings. I can't just dive in and hope for the best. Hell, Noah, I don't even know you."

"You know me."

She shook her head. "I know you here. I could probably almost imagine I could have you here. But then you go back, and you disappear."

Dulcy could see the struggle in him. Could almost hear the protests, the protections. She understood them better than anybody, even if she didn't know why. She just knew that until Noah allowed her past, there would be no more for them.

Somehow she couldn't think of the fact that in the daylight she would remember quickly enough that there would be no more for them, anyway.

"I'm only real here," he said, his voice carrying that odd, haunting need she only heard in the darkness. "I think I could be real with you."

"You think."

His smile was so tentative. "You think this isn't scaring me, too? No matter what you imagine, I'm not like this, either."

Dulcy couldn't help but laugh, a brittle sound. "In that case, Noah, I think we're both in real trouble."

"I know it." He watched her a moment, his eyes dark and hidden, his hands as certain as morning. A man with secrets, with passions Dulcy had only tasted. A man she yearned for without knowing.

He held her there before him as if that contact could ground his words. "I don't know what to do about this," he admitted. "I want to be so careful, because I don't want to hurt you, but I can't seem to stop. I can't keep my hands off you. I can't sleep in the same house with you, and I can't seem to manage the simple walk down to the foreman's house."

As if that should make Dulcy's heart slow down or her throat open again to air. "As simple as that? I hate to tell you, Noah. Life doesn't come in packages that are that neat. I know. I'm the one with a daughter no man would claim and a town full of people who haven't decided to forgive me yet. If I commit to something, I do it completely. I expect it in return. And I expect it to include Hannah as unconditionally as it does me. You want all that? Because if you're serious, that's the only way I come."

Above them the tree whispered. Off in the distance insects throbbed and a dog barked. There, before her in the darkness, Noah seemed to almost shift as he fought something in him to answer.

"You don't understand, do you?" he asked, his voice suddenly so quiet. "What you have with Hannah is one of the reasons I'm falling in love with you."

Dulcy jerked out of his grasp. "Don't say that."

"Why? It's true. Don't you realize how special you are?"

"I'm no different from a million other women who found themselves in my situation."

"You really don't see it." He reached out a tentative hand to test the curve of cheek with his fingers. "My God, Dulcy, Hannah's a marvel. She's bright and unique and blessed with the most honest mouth in Montana. And you're the single person responsible for it."

Dulcy tried so hard not to look at him, not to feel the approval in his eyes. She pulled away, just a little. Just beyond the reach of his hand, so he couldn't hurt her. "I did what I had to."

"No, you didn't. You did what nobody wanted you to. You gave everything to that little girl so she'd feel safe and secure and capable of doing anything. You kept her, you fought for her. You protected her when it would have been so much easier to give in. To drink away the stress or leave her with friends, or forget she was there when you had gentlemen in."

Dulcy's heart caught. Her gaze rose to meet his. She was stunned to stillness. Not by his words. By the sore weight of his voice. By the old grief in his eyes.

It was there. The hollow center to his easy presence, the darkness that hovered at the edge of those commanding eyes.

He stopped so suddenly that the night crept back in. Dulcy heard a radio somewhere, an animal rustle in the distance. She heard the brush of the breeze against her face. She saw the sharp surprise take hold in Noah's eyes. Quick discomfort that grew to shame and then dread.

Dread, as if she could shatter him with a word.

Dulcy couldn't speak past her own surprise, knowing somehow that Noah had never meant to admit what he had. Knowing just as surely that there was more.

He took a breath, never looking away.

"You would have tried your best, I think," he said, his voice so soft and sore and lost. Hesitant with the task of telling. "Even with a husband. But if you were young and frightened and poor, you might have just given in to the anger. Run away and kept running, blaming the one person you could in the whole mess, because he couldn't fight back. You might have finally even left him, because you just didn't know what else to do."

Dulcy was shaking. Humbled. Hurting for the lonely child she suddenly saw in this proud man. She wanted to hold him, to gentle this place in him. She wanted so much to give him back his laughter. She didn't know how, and that hurt the worst.

"You made Hannah proud of who she is," he said simply, and broke her heart for good.

Dulcy didn't know how to answer. Not the gift, not the pain, not the revelation. Words had never been her strong suit, especially when emotions overwhelmed. If it had been Hannah whose eyes she saw open and hurting and needy like this, she would have cradled her in her arms, sung silly songs, murmured in those peculiar mother-tones that eased both parent and child away from the pain.

Dulcy could do none of those things for this man who had never known them. So she raised herself up on her toes, and she kissed him. She lifted her hands to his face, holding it to her, holding him to her.

For just a moment he stood there, frozen, unresponding. Brittle and unyielding as hard glass. Trembling.

Trembling.

And then, as if it were the most normal thing in the world, he wrapped his arms around her and returned the kiss. And Dulcy knew that no matter what else happened, it was too late to go back.

She loved him. She would always love him. Deep in those places a woman keeps secret, where love wars with reality, where commitments are made without the brain's agreement, she knew. She would make love to this man who so enchanted her, so tormented her, so confused her. She would give him what she'd given no man, her woman's heart. And she would regret it to the day she died, because she still didn't believe he could really love her back.

Dulcy wasn't sure how she heard it, not with her pulse thundering in her ears and Noah's hands on her. Protective instincts died hard, though.

The bunkhouse door. The sound of boots on a wooden front porch and Josh's petulant voice complaining about something to one of the other men.

The very thing Dulcy had feared from the moment Noah had opened his eyes. Discovery. Misunderstanding. A lightning-fast jump to conclusions that would end not only her authority but her peace of mind.

Dulcy yanked back, pulling away so fast she almost fell over. She looked up to find Noah's eyes dark and his breathing fast.

"I'm sorry," she whispered, hand to her own chest as if she could stem her sense of loss.

He nodded, lifted a hand. Almost touched her cheek. "It's okay. I understand."

She almost couldn't pull away from his gaze. Couldn't run the way she should. She did, though, making sure Josh hadn't seen them. She ran up to her room and shut herself in and spent another night awake and shivering with a need she hadn't even known she had.

# Ten

---

There was a storm building in the mountains. Noah could hear it muttering in the distance as he swung down off Doofus. The trees had begun to writhe with a fretful, humid wind, and the birds were chattering like impatient women. The horses nickered and danced as the hands led them into the barn.

It had been a long week. After taking three days to get the majority of the herd up to summer pasture, they had ridden fences and repaired irrigation and harvested hay. They'd gone searching for the three young bulls that had been rustled from another pasture while they'd been fixing the fences by Wilson Creek Road.

Noah was tired, and he was sore, and he was anxious for more reasons than he could name. Ethan had been trying to get in touch with him. Noah had ignored him for the last four days. He knew he couldn't much longer. Ethan wasn't the kind to just call and chat.

It didn't matter. Noah didn't want to set as much as a toe back into that world until he had this one settled.

At least until he had it figured out.

He had to tell her. That was the only honest thing to do. He
had to pull her aside somewhere they'd be safe from prying eyes
and admit who he really was.

He had to take the chance.

Until he did, the rest of what they'd shared, what he was
feeling, didn't count.

But every time he tried, other words came out. Funny words,
or silly words, or pointless words. Any words but the ones that
would once again make Noah Campbell invisible.

"You know where the boss is?" he yelled over to Hank where
he was helping get other animals in before the weather hit.

"Cow barn!" Hank yelled.

They'd found something up in the western grazing area Dulcy
should see. A running iron and an old fire. Tools of careful
rustlers. Sitting a hundred yards or so from Cletus Wilson's
land.

Noah put Doofus away and then headed over to the cow
barn, pulling off gloves and hat as he went. It was hot enough
to fry eggs on his forehead. Sweat dripped down his back and
under his arms. Noah wiped his forehead with the back of his
arm and pushed dank hair out of his eyes. The afternoon was
just too hot, and the animal life too unsettled. Almost as unsettled as he was.

"Dulcy?"

The barn seemed even more dim. Noah heard the animals
shifting inside, smelled the hay and cattle and old leather. He
heard a voice and followed it back.

"Hello?"

A cow lowed, an anxious, unhappy sound. Noah saw it at the
back of the barn. Saw it bump against the wall and back
around. He saw the shadowy form of someone crouched
alongside it.

Someone who wasn't Dulcy.

He stepped farther in and realized it was a man. It was a man
he didn't know.

A man who was bent over Dulcy's prone form on the floor.

Only she wasn't prone. She was reclining, her head on a
couple bales of hay, her legs stretched out. The guy's hands
were on her shoulders, and his head was right over hers.

"How's that feel, honey?" he was asking in low tones.

Noah wasn't sure what happened. Later he might admit that he let other functions override simple logic. All he knew at that moment was that he was hit with a rage that sent him careening into them both.

"What the hell do you think you're doing!" he roared, spinning the man around.

In a flash he saw Dulcy's eyes snap open like flags on a high breeze. He saw her hand on her chest, just as it had been the other night when she'd pulled away from him. He saw the confusion in the man's eyes.

The handsome, young man's eyes.

And he swung.

The man howled and went over. Noah howled and spun the other way.

"Oh, damn!" He shook his hand in astonishment, the sudden pain clearing his head. "That hurt!"

"You sound surprised," the other guy responded from the floor where he was rubbing his jaw.

Noah glared at him. "Who the hell are you?"

"The victim, I think," he answered without moving.

"The vet," Dulcy amended in a small voice from where she hadn't moved.

"The vet?" Noah all but howled again, spinning on her.

That was when he realized what was wrong. Dulcy didn't look rapturous. She looked uncomfortable. And she wasn't touching her chest, she was rubbing it.

The rest of the rage cleared away in an appalling instant, and Noah realized that he, the man who had climbed to improbable success by always keeping his head, had just lost it. Again.

"I hit him for nothing, didn't I?" he asked her, feeling the flush climb his neck.

Dulcy grinned, still breathing funny. "Don't you know not to punch anybody with your thumb inside your fist? It's a great way to break your hand."

Noah's answering grin was pretty sheepish. "Now you tell me." He took another considering look at his reddened knuckles and then reached out to give his victim a hand up. "I've never done that before."

"Never?" Dulcy echoed.

He scowled as he helped resettle the vet on his feet. "Does that mean you don't love me anymore?"

She continued to gently rub at her sternum. "No, not at all. I'm thrilled that when you belatedly came to violence in your life, it was over me. I would have preferred you didn't cold-cock the vet, though."

Noah turned a chagrined glance at the other injured party. "Which means that there's a perfectly reasonable explanation for all this."

The vet nodded and held out a hand. "I'm afraid so. Jim Peterson."

Noah shook hands. "Noah Campbell."

Peterson grinned. "I know. I was in Lone Star your first night here. I don't think you remember."

Another point against him. "Your way of telling me I have nothing to say to a woman who likes to lie in the straw with cows, I guess."

"Cows who kick," Dulcy explained gingerly, still not moving.

Noah turned on her, now really upset. "She kicked you?"

Dulcy waved a hand. "It's only fair. I was shoving a syringe up her teat."

"You want to sit up now, Dulce?" Peterson asked.

"I don't know." She shot Noah a wary look. "If I do, are you going to hit me?"

Noah bit back an oath. "I'm sorry. I really am. I thought he was hurting you."

Her eyes were getting brighter by the minute. "Uh-huh."

"*Are* you okay?"

"Yeah. Just got the wind knocked out of me. Jim's got some interesting news you should hear."

"Oh. Good." Noah felt like an idiot. A randy, rutting teen who went into shutdown the minute a woman looked at him.

He couldn't help it. He wasn't getting any sleep, any peace at all. He'd spent three days out in the sun and wind with Dulcy and slept alongside her out in the mountains without being able to touch her. He'd let her send him to do busy work just so he wouldn't be too close. So he couldn't smell her and see her and listen to her throaty, full laugh.

He'd sated himself on their small moments together and tormented himself with his deception.

"You ready to get up?" Jim Peterson asked Dulcy.

"Yeah." She took Jim's hand, when Noah was too preoccupied to react quickly enough, and levered herself to her feet, still rubbing. "Ethan called while you were out. He's beginning to sound annoyed."

"He'll wait," Noah said, and realized how annoyed *he* was beginning to sound. "I have something to share with you, too. We found a running iron out by Cletus's place."

The three of them headed back out of the barn, Dulcy already shaking her head. "It's not Cletus. Jim found some of our cattle."

Noah pushed open the door and ushered them all out to find the storm even closer. The wind had picked up, piling the clouds higher along the western peaks. Dulcy looked up, her eyes assessing, her nostrils twitching with the smell of the storm, her ears sorting out trouble.

Noah wanted to photograph her that way, with the uncertain light sinking into those crystal eyes and limning her hair with fire. He wanted to wrap himself in that lustrous hair and sink into her mouth. He wanted good-looking Jim Peterson to take his black bag somewhere else. Hell, preferably.

God, he thought in near despair. It was time to either get the hell away or get Dulcy into bed, and he couldn't do either.

"Head on into the house," Dulcy suggested, a hand out to each of them. "I need to make sure Hank has everything battened down."

The three of them battened together, getting animals secured and buildings closed up. Out behind the house, Sally was yanking sheets off the line, and Hannah was pulling in her toys, oblivious to the sudden crack of thunder that ricocheted along the valley.

A storm was brewing. Noah knew just how the atmosphere felt. Itchy and unsettled and anxious. Waiting, sensing, splintering with the harnessed energy that was about to be unleashed.

He wiped at his forehead and found that he wasn't any cooler, no matter what the wind was doing.

* * *

"Where'd he find the cattle?" Noah asked.

They stood in the kitchen like strangers, waiting for the storm. It was the last place Dulcy wanted to be, at least alone with Noah. Sally had taken Hannah back with her to batten down the Bixby house, and Jim had been called away to a horse who had reacted to the lightning with a lunge into barbed wire.

The sky was divided into unequal halves, with the black, thick-bellied clouds shoving out the blue, and the thunder rolling right down the mountains. The bursts of wind were chilly, and the air smelled like lightning. It was almost dark at four in the afternoon.

"Well," Dulcy said, fumbling through a cabinet for a glass and pouring herself a slug of water. "I asked Jim to check with his contacts around the state. Anybody seeing what might be a Lazy V bull going up for auction. You wouldn't steal bulls to slaughter," she explained. "Not ours, anyway. They're champion stock."

Noah nodded and Dulcy turned away. It was the storm. Stirring everything up, spinning it around. Skittering along her nerve endings with each shudder of approaching lightning, each surprise clap of thunder.

That was why she couldn't sit still in here with him. That was why she wanted to touch him.

It was exactly why she shouldn't.

Dulcy saw it on Noah, too. A stiffness, an uncertainty, as if he'd never set foot in her kitchen before or allowed himself to be alone with a woman. They were discussing business as if they were in a roomful of accountants, and that was the last thing either of them was thinking about.

Dulcy finished her water and poured a second glass, wishing she could just pour it over her head. "Jim said that one of his friends called from Miles City. That's about three hundred miles away. He's pretty sure he saw a couple of our bulls up there. Says he knows the rancher who put 'em up, and he'd never seen stock that good from his ranch in his life."

"Anybody we know?"

She shook her head. "I'm getting the information to Bart for you so he can check it out."

Noah kept fussing with the collar of his shirt, as if it were too tight. "Any ideas who our rustlers are?"

"Nope." Dulcy wanted to fight her own clothes. It was so thick in this room. Breathless with waiting. "You've seen the evidence. They're not disappearing from just one place, like it might be a nearby neighbor. We've seen tire tracks and horse tracks, so it's not one type of conveyance. Uncle Mike has lost about ten head, and Bob Wilson about fifteen. I'm hoping the men we put up in the old line shack with the herd can watch 'em for now so we don't lose any more."

"Do you think that's why I was shot at?"

"I'd sure rather it be that than just somebody trying to shoot you so they could get the ranch."

"Whose ranch borders the area I was riding?"

"Cletus Wilson. But it wouldn't be Cletus."

"Why not? That's where we found the running iron."

Dulcy turned on him, the empty glass tight in her hands, her first instinct to blindly defend her neighbors against this stranger. Then she saw him, saw those sweet eyes, that tight jaw that gave away so little, and knew he was no stranger.

She ended up giving him a self-effacing grin. "I don't want it to be. I like him."

"Anybody you don't like?"

Dulcy laughed at that. "Sure. But I would have thought I'd have had an inkling of who it might be."

Noah looked away, looked back again. "What about Josh?"

"What about him?"

"Would he be mad enough at you to try and get you fired?"

Dulcy walked to the window and stared out at the barns, where dust was twirling in the air and the automatic lights had come on. "Sure. I'm not sure he's smart enough to sabotage a computer, though."

"Who else uses them?"

She shrugged. "Just about everybody. We're hooked into half the businesses in town and the county agent. Makes ordering a heck of a lot easier, not to mention bill paying. Most everybody's doing it that way now."

"Well, that narrows it down."

"Which is why I've been tearing my hair out since you showed up."

"Do you think it's personal?"

Dulcy fought the urge to look at him, because if she did, she couldn't think. She couldn't reason, which was what they needed right now. For more reasons than busting a rustler. "It could be. You've seen how people react to my having this position. But you also have to consider the fact that you have some of the best acreage in the area. And some of the best beef. Not to mention the fact that Aunt Cordelia played this valley like an accordion when she decided to sell the ranch."

Behind her, Noah shifted. Walked a couple of paces. Rubbed at the sweat on his chest. Dulcy could hear him, could see him too-well-reflected in the window.

"What about Hank?"

That got her around. "What about him?"

Noah faced her calmly. "All I heard in town was why Hank wasn't manager. Why isn't he?"

"Because I'm better. Because he doesn't want anything to do with computers. Because we work well just the way we are. He's the stockman and I'm the technician."

"You're sure."

She smiled. "Yes. Hank is much happier out on a horse than stuck up here staring at numbers all day."

"Leaves us right back where we started."

"Call Ethan."

"After the storm."

As if summoned, a bolt of lightning split the sky into sparks and the house lights flickered. Thunder shook the windows. The storm was breaking. If Dulcy walked to the front of the house, she could watch the rain dim the mountains and then march across the valley. She could watch the lightning splinter across the sky. She could feel that lovely cool wind on her face.

She started walking before she thought about it. Noah followed right on her heels.

"How are you feeling?" he asked, as if it were perfectly natural to just bolt in the middle of a conversation.

"Fine."

Dulcy reached the living room and opened the big door. The wind shoved its way past the screen door like an impatient child, battering at her face and rippling across her shirt. It should have cooled her, comforted her. Noah walked up right behind her and took all that away.

"You sure?" he asked, his voice gentle with concern. "You're walking like you're an arm short."

Dulcy didn't turn away from where the mountains had disappeared through the screen door. "I'm a little stiff. Petula's bigger than I am."

Noah's laugh was a burst of air against her neck. "Petula? You named a cow Petula?"

She couldn't help but smile. "Hannah named a cow Petula."

He laid his hands on her shoulders and she damn near bolted in the other direction. "Settle down," he soothed in a voice like butter. "If there's one thing I've been able to indulge in, in that fast track of mine, it's a good masseur."

Dulcy wanted to shiver. She wanted to fold up, just under the weight of two callused, square hands. "You're sending for him?"

"He taught me some tricks. Now relax."

It was the oldest come-on in the world. Dulcy knew it. Noah knew it. The problem was he kneaded the taut line of her neck and shoulders into pudding and then stopped.

Stopped!

Dulcy almost screamed at him. Outside, the rain had arrived, blowing in fitful gusts right through the screen door so that it beaded on her cheeks. The valley shuddered and swayed, buffeted by wind and thunder and rain. In that echoing, still room in a darkened house, Dulcy stood rigid and frustrated, exhilarated by the storm, by the sweet honey somebody had just poured all through her muscles, by Noah's proximity, and yet unable to do anything about it.

She knew it was wrong. It was stupid, it was shortsighted, it was self-destructive. She hadn't let a man near her in seven years, and she'd done well. She knew every reason she shouldn't let this man near her today, and yet for the life of her she couldn't make one reason stand out enough to be noticed past the quicksilver his fingers had unleashed in her. Past the laughter and the silences and the revelations she'd never expected.

"Noah?"

"Yes, Dulcy."

God, his voice was tight as a bowstring. How could his hands be so relaxed on her shoulders? Could he be that much of a gentleman that he would control himself to the point she wouldn't know how he was affected?

"You're a very good masseur."

"Thank you."

The wind spun the trees and made them bend. Dulcy felt as if it were doing the same to her. "There's a problem, though."

"Uh-huh?"

"I'm not relaxed."

Pause. "You're not?"

"No." Breath. Courage. "I'm not."

He never moved. Still, Dulcy could feel the same moment of hesitation in him, the same gathering of purpose. "Is there something I can do about it?"

She smiled a woman's smile he couldn't even see. She battled a terrible headiness. "Well . . . I'm all hot and sweaty."

His hands tightened, just a little. His voice was even smaller. "Yes?"

"Are you . . . hot and sweaty?"

"Yes," he admitted as another gust of rain spattered them both. "I think I am."

Dulcy was trembling now. Frightened and hungry and committed. "Do you think a shower would help?"

He groaned. Dulcy heard it and almost went slack beneath him. She never got the chance. Before she could so much as flinch, Noah spun her around and had her in his arms. He brought his mouth down to hers and his hands so tight around her she couldn't breathe, anyway.

It all ended. All the sanity, all the defenses, all the protest died in that single kiss. In the span of Noah's arms. Dulcy never had the chance to make up her mind about what was going to happen, because it happened anyway.

She should have run. Instead, she reached up. She caught her hands in his hair and pulled him hard to her. She opened to his kiss, tasting impatience and fire and need in the deep recesses of his quirky mouth. She arched against him so that her breasts were crushed against his chest, so his hands could find her, so he could pull her shirt off and she could feel his skin next to her.

He didn't pull off her shirt. He pulled out her hair tie. He wound her hair around his fingers and pulled the braid apart. He fanned her hair behind her like a sunset and sent cascades of delight down her back with his touch. He commanded her with his mouth and seduced her with his touch.

His beard chafed her cheek, so she lifted fingers to rub against it. His hands chafed her neck, so she rubbed against them. His neck was slick with sweat, so she tasted it.

"I don't think . . ." he managed to say, pulling at her shirt to get it out of her jeans, "we're going to make that shower yet."

Dulcy yanked back, suddenly so hungry for the feel of his skin she couldn't breathe. "I think you're right."

His chest was hard, sculpted, glistening. Dulcy kissed it, kissed his throat, his jaw. She lifted high on her toes to rediscover his mouth, but he had other ideas. He swept her up in his arms and turned for the stairs.

"My room," she rasped, arms tight around his neck. "Bigger bed."

"My room," he retorted, dipping to make another meal of her lower lip. "Supplies."

Dulcy should have been appalled. With him. With herself. She chuckled, a throaty sound of delight that propelled Noah even faster up the stairs. Up the dim stairs where the lightning licked the walls and the thunder added an urgent rhythm. Back to his room where a four-poster sat in front of the window and Noah laid Dulcy down.

He somehow turned pulling off her boots into an erotic art. He swept impatient hands up her legs and beyond, to where he could pull off her belt and unbutton her fly. Dulcy shuddered with his touch. She reached up to reclaim his arms, his hard, well-worked shoulders. Noah took hold of her hands and lifted them over her head. He ran his hands up her waist, her sides, her arms. He finished lifting her shirt out of her jeans and bent back to unbutton it.

"Poor Dulcy," he murmured against her throat. "You're getting a bruise."

And then he kissed it. He claimed another button, and another, his mouth following, tasting her right through her work clothes, too impatient to wait. Dulcy began to writhe, the storm building in her, gathering with his touch, with his deliberate, maddening seduction. She batted away his hands and reached down to test the strength of his denim.

"Oh, God," Noah groaned, eyes closed. "That's not fair."

Dulcy showed him how fair she was by popping his button.

Suddenly she had on only her jeans. She reacted instinctively, reaching down to cover herself. Noah grabbed hold of her hands and smiled.

He smiled, and Dulcy forgot what she'd thought she didn't want him to see.

"You're beautiful," he whispered, cupping one breast. Tasting the tender underside with tongue and teeth. Sending her almost straight off the bed. "I've been thinking...of this..."

Dulcy had, too. But not like this. Never this good, this sweet, this hot. Noah closed his mouth over her breast and she cried out. He flattened his hand across her belly and she moved against him, hungry and hurting with impatience.

The thunder growled and Noah tasted her other breast, the wet trail of his mouth lighting fires in her. Striking lightning. Dulcy whimpered, bucked, reached for him. She teased her fingers with the soft hair that dusted the vee of his throat and darkened his chest. She followed it as it tapered to his belly, his flat, hard belly that beckoned her. She tasted when she could, too. She thought how delicious hard work and open air was, how the smell of lightning in the air was as hedonistic as liquor.

Noah slipped his hand beneath her open jeans, beneath her practical cotton panties. Dulcy couldn't hold still. She wanted her clothes off, but she didn't, the feel of his hand beneath that very proper denim dangerous and forbidden.

His fingers sought, dipped, stroked, and she cried out. She wept with want and danced with desire. After interminable hibernation, her body sang with life, with sensation, with the delicious power of being coveted.

Dulcy couldn't wait any longer. She pulled her jeans off herself. And then she made sure Noah paid for his torment by raising the simple unzipping of a zipper to new and excruciating levels of delight. Noah was laughing and cursing at the same time, his body slick with strain, his eyes dark and deep, his smile knowing.

"*You're* beautiful," Dulcy couldn't help but say, her eyes following her hands across him, up and down him. He had new tan lines, new scrapes and bruises that she kissed and tasted and touched. He had harder edges to his muscles and a flatter ridge to his abdomen. She explored it all with quick hands and hungry eyes. She saw what she did to him and smiled a secret smile.

And then Noah took charge. He took hold of her hands in his, silenced her mouth with his, covered her body with his and eased his way back with clever fingers to find her slick and ready. He tormented her, delighted her, spun her around and sent her flying with just his fingers, his fingers and his delightful, cunning mouth.

And when he urged her open with his whispers and his questing hands, she welcomed him, took her fill of him, wrapped herself around him and urged him closer, closer, until he was gasping and she was sobbing, and the world spun apart around them in the rain and the lightning and the wind.

The storm must have passed. A shaft of molten sun drizzled down the far wall, and the birds had started to chatter again. Dulcy lay wrapped in Noah's arms and couldn't move. She couldn't think what to do past this moment when everything seemed so right. When her body, for the first time in her life, told her what lovemaking really was.

"Wanna take that shower now?" Noah asked, tickling her breast with a lock of her own hair.

Dulcy couldn't even muster the energy to protest. "Whenever."

She felt liquid, warm and complacent and sated. She felt unique. The light crept across the tumbled white sheet where it lay gathered below Noah's waist, and Dulcy bided her time considering the delicious properties of light and form and substance. Especially substance.

"Would it sound too hokey if I said it's never been like this before?" he asked.

She chuckled. "Absolutely. I *can* say it, though, since my one and only real experience was at fifteen."

Noah lifted his head and looked at her. "I thought you said you were a regular tart."

Dulcy gave him a crooked smile. "I said everybody *thought* I was a regular tart. My experience is limited. My learning curve, however, is exceptional."

"Which means what?"

*Which means I shouldn't be here. I shouldn't feel so happy, so loved, so complete.*

"Which means," she said instead, nestling a little closer, "that I'm glad you were considerate enough to bring your party favors."

It was his turn to chuckle. "No gentleman would ask a lady to dance without bringing his good shoes."

Dulcy knew that he was avoiding the next moment, too. It should have made her angry, frightened. Something. She knew that would all come in time, probably right in line before *disillusioned, desolate* and *resigned.* But for now the sunlight was golden and Noah was the one man who could rewrite her history.

That would, of course, be when the back door slammed. "Dulcy!"

Dulcy jerked up as if she'd been hit with a live wire.

Josh.

God, of all people to wander into the kitchen, of all times.

"Ignore him," Noah all but begged. "He'll go away."

Dulcy groaned. "No, he won't. He knows we're here."

She swung out of bed and fumbled for her clothes, the delight she'd carried in her chest curdling hard. She felt like a cheating wife, like a stupid schoolgirl caught behind the bleachers. She felt like every foolish woman who'd let her hormones get the better of her.

"Dulcy, where are you? We got problems at the feed store!"

"I'm coming, Josh!"

Dulcy got her shirt buttoned and spun for the door, leaving Noah behind to pull himself together. She had already reached the bottom of the steps before she realized what she'd forgotten. What Josh would notice right away. What would send her reputation right back to hell.

She'd forgotten her hair.

In all the time she'd been here she had never been seen in anything but that tight braid, except at the dance the week before. She certainly wouldn't let her hair down in the middle of a working day. And it wouldn't look fingered and tousled and damp.

Dulcy realized her mistake the minute Josh caught sight of her. His expression went from sullen to furious and from there to triumphant.

"Well," he said in that pressed little voice that sounded so much like his mother's. "That didn't take long."

"What's wrong at the feed store?" she asked, walking right by him, even though she knew darn well it was too late to take the high road. By eight o'clock tonight the entire town would know. Even if Noah called every one of them out, it would be too late.

Josh followed her back into the kitchen, his boots clacking on the floor. "What's wrong is that I couldn't get the order, because the bank account's been closed." She heard that first smile in his voice, the first smirk. "Is that part of the plan?"

Dulcy was fighting so hard not to hit him. She walked to the refrigerator and got herself a cold soda. Took a minute to pop it before answering, her voice deceptively quiet. "Exactly what did they say at the feed store?"

"Same thing they said at the mercantile and the repair shop. We can't draw on your account because you closed it yesterday. But then, now that I see what's going on, I imagine you knew already. What was it going to be, Rio or the Caribbean?"

"Thank you for telling me about the bank, Josh. I'll take care of it. You can get back to work now."

"And what about you?" he asked, his words a feral snarl. "You gonna get back to work now, too?"

She lost the fight. It probably didn't hurt Josh as much as it was going to hurt her, but Dulcy put her soda down on the counter and carefully curled her thumb around the outside of her fist. And then she hit Josh squarely across the jaw.

"Never mind getting back to work," she informed him where he sat stunned on the floor. "Get out. I'll send your pay wherever you want it. Just not here."

"You'll regret this," he blustered, stumbling to his feet.

Dulcy laughed. "Been there, done that," she said, dismissing him.

Even though she knew she would. Not the hit. The mistake. The terrible mistake that still thrummed along her arms and legs and settled in her deepest places with a warmth that shouldn't have made her cry.

Ten minutes ago she'd felt that everything had been possible. Now she knew better. It was over instead.

# Eleven

---

"Dulcy?"

She didn't bother to move from where she was sitting at the computer. "You'd better call Ethan."

Noah walked up right behind her and let his fingers stray to her hair. Dulcy pulled away. His touch was just too intimate, too familiar. Dulcy was having too much trouble controlling her tears as it was.

Noah walked around to where she could see him and knelt down at eye level. She loved his eyes. They were so dear, so alive, so compelling. They could tell her so much before he ever spoke.

She couldn't bear to see what they were telling her now, so she faced the information on her screen.

"I'll kill him," Noah said, and she knew he meant it.

"Two acts of violence in the same day," she responded, still not facing him, her voice as tight as her chest. "I'm a great influence on you. I'm about to get Mr. Grumman from the bank on the phone up here. Our accounts were all closed. You might want to call Ethan on the house line and see if that's what he's been trying to call and tell you about."

"Damn Ethan," he snapped, grabbing her arm. "Talk to me."

Dulcy tried so hard to be reasonable. To be logical and strong. She couldn't when he was this close, when the tears clogged her throat with useless recriminations. So she pulled away from him. "I have to do this now, Noah. Please. We'll talk later."

"Then we'll do it together. Get the bank on the phone. I'll wait."

It took her three tries to dial the right number. Her fingers wouldn't work. Her voice wasn't doing much better. In the end she got the answers for her call to Ethan. Dulcy knew how hard it was for Noah to do, but he walked on downstairs to listen on the other line. She thought that was the first breath she'd taken since Josh had slammed out of the house.

"Well, what the hell have you two been up to?" Ethan demanded. "I've been trying to get you for four days."

The silence was taut and damning. Finally it was Noah who managed to participate. "Taking the herd up to summer pasture. Now, what the hell's going on?"

"Somebody's been siphoning money out of your account again, that's what. We closed it before anything else could happen."

"That account was brand new," Dulcy protested. "We changed it all when this happened the last time. You signed the papers."

"And I probably would have liked to know the real reason you changed everything over," he retorted.

"That's not a topic of discussion," Noah said with a finality that brought silence from the other end.

"Okay."

"We set up elaborate safety measures in the computer system," Dulcy continued. "Mr. Grumman swore we wouldn't have any more trouble."

"Unless somebody knew the safety measures."

Dulcy knew she should be thinking about that. She couldn't pull anything together past the fact that Noah's scent still clung to her skin. She could still hear his laughter, his surprised sighs of delight.

She should have known better. She should still know better. She should just quit the damn job and work for a rodeo.

"Dulcy? Any ideas?"

"Oh . . . um, I haven't seen any conspicuous consumption around here recently. Can you trace any of it anywhere?"

"Not really."

"You want to ask your Aunt Cordelia who she *didn't* sell this ranch to, Dulcy?" Noah asked. "That might be a shorter suspect list."

"Okay," she acknowledged, trying so hard to get her brain to work, to push its way past the last few minutes, the last few hours. She squeezed her eyes shut and rubbed at them, trying to force away the ache of tears. "Uh, how 'bout we work with Bart Bixby and Mr. Grumman to check the bank's records. See if the discrepancy might show up anywhere else. A mistake or maybe a cranky employee."

"Who's Bart Bixby?"

"Sheriff."

This time the pause was telling. "You sure you want to involve him?"

The same question everyone in town would ask. For the very same reason.

"Apologize, Ethan," Noah suggested in steely tones.

"I'm not saying it's Dulcy. She stopped it the last time."

"Okay," Dulcy said, rubbing a couple of fingers between her eyes. "For now, let's do this. Accounts are closed. I'll call all the businesses tomorrow and say we're going back to the normal method of business. The town'll be thrilled. It considers itself progressive as hell for hooking into this system."

"It is," Ethan assured her. "It just has a good hacker screwing it up. You want me to deal with the banker?"

"Please. He's a nice man, but he's not real fond of me."

"Who's he related to?" Noah asked.

Dulcy could almost afford him a smile. "Actually, he's not related to me. He's Walt Stewart's nephew. Doesn't matter, though. Since I'm the one who talked the town into computerizing in the first place, he might as well be Aunt Mary herself."

"You did that?" Ethan demanded.

"Yep. I guess I just figured it was a lot easier to embezzle the town's money that way. Only I just stole Noah's."

"Dulcy, stop it," Noah snapped. "Let's get on it, Ethan. I'll start playing on the computer from here."

"No, you won't," Ethan disagreed. "You're going to call your friend Marshall."

"Marshall?" Noah retorted, suddenly sounding cautious. "Why?"

"Because something went wrong and he needs you back. Right now. He's been driving me nuts."

"Wrong? Wrong? There shouldn't be anything wrong. I busted my ass on that!"

"Talk to him about it," Ethan suggested dryly. "I'm just the messenger. I'll talk to you tomorrow, Dulcy."

Dulcy hung up the phone and stared at it. Stared at the screen. Thought about what was coming and wondered where the heck she was going to get the strength to go through this all over again. Wondered what she was going to do to protect Hannah from it.

Hannah. Oh, God, what was going to happen to her baby? What was going to happen to them both?

Dulcy sat at her desk and stared down the road that stretched over the valley. Pretty soon Sally's compact would top the rise that led to the front gate. She and Hannah would be back, full of news about the storm, full of enthusiasm and noise. Full of life. Dulcy watched and waited and ignored the raised voice from the floor below, where Noah was arguing with somebody named Marshall about a screwup in production scheduling. She watched the sun settle behind another bank of clouds to the west and the shadows slide east. She listened to the birds and the cattle and the distant water, and she thought she was going to die without it.

And she knew it was going to get worse. Because she wouldn't only lose the ranch. She'd end up losing Noah, too.

"Dulcy?"

She didn't turn. "I think I'm going to have to leave. Would you like me to train Hank before I go?"

Noah crouched before her, a hand on hers. "You're not going anywhere."

She tried to draw breath and ended up making an awful, sobbing sound. "I just can't go through it again."

"I'll take care of it," he objected, cradling her hands in his. "I'll go into town—"

"No!" She turned to see the pain in those soft gray eyes, and it made her hurt all the worse. "Don't do that."

"But, Dulcy, I can't let Josh get away with this."

"No, Noah. Don't you see? It would only make it worse."

"Tell me how."

Dulcy wanted to smile for him, to lessen the impact of her words. "People are funny. They believe what they want. And if you went around town defending my honor against the truth, people would just be all the more convinced that Josh is right. That I'm a scheming bitch who's doing her best to take all your money and thumb my nose at the people who knew better all along. Besides, don't you have to get back to work?"

"There's no way I'm leaving you right now."

"Ethan and I will work it out. I promise. If you want to make people think you trust me absolutely, going about your business is the best argument." She saw him begin to protest. "Really."

"We need some time, Dulcy," he insisted, his face taut with distress. "Just you and me. I need to explain some things."

"You don't need to explain anything to me."

Dulcy laughed, but it sounded as sore as Dulcy's heart. "Oh, yes I do. I'm a coward, because I won't do it now. But I want to tell you when we can focus on just that. On just us."

Just us. How could it possibly hurt worse? "You're married in that other life and your wife has a big ax?" Dulcy asked, trying so hard to be lighthearted.

His smile took it all away. It was the saddest, loneliest smile she'd ever seen. "No," he answered, rubbing at her hands with gentle fingers. "No wife. We'll get through this, Dulcy. I promise."

Dulcy almost ran right out the door just on the weight of those two words. Dulcy had been promised before. By selfish people, by sincere people, by people who walked in righteousness. She thought she'd never wanted to believe a promise as much before in her life. But she didn't remember how anymore.

"Okay."

"You won't do anything stupid while I'm gone, like walk out?"

Dulcy did manage a smile this time, although it cost her more than almost anything she'd done in her life. "Now, why would I do something like that?"

"I quit, Hank," she said three days later.

"You can't let people run you off this ranch," Hank protested.

"I can't let them hurt Hannah anymore. This afternoon three different people in town refused to talk to her because they were sure I'd set up the computer system to defraud the valley. Somebody else threw a rock through the windshield while we were in the bank."

"Aw, Hannah's tougher than you think. She don't wanna leave here."

"Neither do I. But I just don't think I have a choice."

"And that little girl? What are you gonna do with her?"

"She's having a vacation with Sally's parents."

"So, you're not tellin' her she ain't comin' back."

"Not yet."

Hank delivered his judgment in absolute silence. If Dulcy weren't already so numb, that would have hurt, too.

She'd finally made her decision the night before, late, when she'd been on the phone again with Ethan. They weren't getting anything accomplished. The call Dulcy had made to Aunt Cordelia had just netted the information that bids for the Lazy V had come in from every rancher in the area and two businesses, Montana Inc. and International Investments Partners, both listed as California corporations, which would have explained on a dime why Aunt Cordelia hadn't sold to them. Noah's bid had come in behind the IIP people, Uncle Mike and, of all people, Cletus Wilson.

Cletus had disavowed any knowledge of the running iron, and the bank any knowledge of where Noah's money had gone. Dulcy's authority at the ranch was disintegrating, and her reputation was in tatters. She decided she had to act before there was nothing left to salvage.

She had to leave before Noah was forced off the land he'd learned to love almost as much as she did. Land, she was beginning to realize, he needed even more.

"I've talked to Mr. Campbell," she told Hank. "He's going to leave things in your hands for right now and find a replacement when one of them can get back to supervise it."

Dulcy didn't bother to tell him which Mr. Campbell. Let Hank think Noah was in on it all.

"I hate that damn computer."

"Let Sally help you."

"What about you? Where are you going?"

Dulcy shrugged. "I don't know. For right now, I'm just going to take a vacation. I'm taking Colorado with me."

"Only fair. You brought him with you."

She'd brought a lot of things with her she didn't have anymore. And she'd found something she'd lost again.

Oh, God, Noah. Noah with his heartbreaking smile and his lonely eyes. Noah who hadn't believed he could fall in love in a week.

You *can* fall in love in a week, Dulcy wanted to tell him. In a day. In a heartbeat—the first time you see a tousled, hung-over, unmade bed of a man open his eyes.

She'd brought her isolation with her when she'd come to the ranch. Her careful common sense and independence. Noah had taken them back home with him, and Dulcy didn't know what to do.

She didn't know what to do but leave, so he could save what was his.


Sally tried to talk Dulcy out of it, too. She didn't have any better luck than Noah had.

"Do you know what you're about to give up?" she demanded, hands on flour-dusted denim-clad hips.

"I'll find another job."

"I'm not talking about the job," Sally insisted, leaning closer, bright blue eyes as intense as Dulcy had ever seen them.

So Dulcy faced her, and Dulcy told her the truth. "Yes," she said simply. "I know. I also know that within ten minutes of stepping off that plane back home, he'll forget just what was so fascinating about the cute little ranch girl he left back in Montana. So I'm not giving up that much, anyway."

"Dulcy, don't be stupid . . ."

"There is one thing," Dulcy said, getting to her feet and reaching for the last of her suitcases rather than face Sally with tears in her eyes. "I like him better with gray eyes."

Dulcy lasted three days before calling Hannah. Four until she called Sally. The person she really needed to talk to was Noah, but she couldn't. Not now. Not yet. It didn't matter that when she managed to catch some sleep she dreamed of him. It didn't matter that she kept expecting to see him when she turned around. It didn't matter that everything she did was to help him find his home. She couldn't tell him.

She took Colorado up and rode the high meadows to work off some of the boredom of sitting in an economy motel at the edge of town. She took her meals in paper bags and did her laundry in the sink. And she worked hard, with only one thing in mind.

Only one.

Noah.

When she walked into town she heard the whispers that she was drinking herself to death in that motel, even though nobody had seen her bring in a bottle. When she called Sally it was to hear that her friends were afraid she was suicidal. When she talked to Hannah, she just laughed and assured her daughter that they were going to try and go home soon.

Some of the people in town did still talk to her, and that was where she gleaned her best information.

"Cletus and his wife are havin' trouble," Miss Etta mourned with a sad shake of the head. "There's a rumor he's seein' a young waitress over from Livingston."

"I heard that Josh finally got hisself a job," the owner of the gas station confided as he collected Dulcy's money. "Workin' for Walt Stewart. You know he's talkin' about you."

Dulcy knew.

"Can you imagine that ole Pete Dunn is learning how to ski?" demanded the owner of the stable where Dulcy had to keep Colorado. "I can just see him on those skinny legs of his, chawin' tobacco, with Vera yellin' at him to get back to the store where he belongs, the old fool. Seems Bob Grumman's been trying to get him to ski for a while, finally did it. Now, of course, Bob can't go because of the problems at the bank, which wouldn't be there if a certain somebody hadn't gone and tried to prove herself smarter than the rest of the world by talking us all into computer billing.''

They weren't necessarily all kind, but they were talkative. Dulcy took all their stories and opinions and information back with her when she sat down with her computer and her modem and her phone to Ethan, who really had the statistical world at his fingertips. And then, far into each night, the two of them tried to find some kind of pattern.

A week later, Dulcy was riding up in the high plains when she came across something interesting. Surveyors. Out in the middle of nowhere. No roads, no public access, no reason to be there. And yet, there they were.

She didn't ask. She just looked around her at the steep slopes, the mantle of pine, the clear, sweet, blue sky. She looked down into the far valley and saw the backside of Westridge. And she wondered if she was right about just whose property she was on.

When she got back to town, the first thing she did was climb in the Jeep and head over to the county courthouse to check plats. She looked up titles and requests and especially the environmental impact studies of the area. Then, smiling for the first time in two weeks, she headed back and talked to Ethan about just who it was who had put in the bids for the Lazy V those months ago and why. And then she called Cletus Wilson's wife and asked her if she could stop by for coffee.

Dulcy heard the phone ring as she stepped out of the shower. After getting back from the Wilsons' she'd put in a call to Ethan. He'd probably gotten the information she needed. She hopped over unpacked suitcases to get to the phone.

"Hello?"

"Hi, Mom. Can you come get me?"

"Hannah?"

"You need to come get her."

Dulcy sat hard on the edge of the bed. The voice wasn't Sally's father's. It wasn't a voice she knew.

"Who is this?" she demanded. "What's going on?"

"What's going on is simple. We have your little girl. If you want to see her, you'll meet with us. If you say a word to your cousin the sheriff, she disappears."

"Please..." Dulcy couldn't make her voice work. She couldn't make her brain work. Hannah. Oh, sweet God, not her baby. "I don't have any money."

"We just want to talk. You have a horse. We'll tell you where to meet us."

"Of course. Anything."

"No police."

"None."

They told her. She listened, even as her heart ran away with her. Even as she fought to keep from running out the door. Noah, she thought instinctively. God, Noah, help, they have my baby.

"Don't hurt her," Dulcy begged, who never begged.

"Behave and we won't. You have two hours."

Dulcy tried to call Sally's parents, but they weren't home. She tried to call Bart, but it was the dispatcher who answered. The dispatcher who'd been known to spread rumors faster than Aunt Mary. She railed over the fact that she couldn't call Noah, but there was no way to get hold of him.

So she called Ethan and left a message before grabbing her keys and running out the door. She didn't even remember to lock up.

Four hours later, a riderless Colorado trotted into the barnyard of the Lazy V and butted a startled Hank for his dinner.

Noah couldn't seem to concentrate. It was a simple scene. All he had to do was kiss the girl and make her cry, something he'd done in at least ten films so far. Something he'd already done in this film three times. He just hadn't done it at the end of the movie, which was what the test audience had wanted him to do. So Marshall Wellman had called the entire cast back for a week's shoot to finish two new scenes and then loop them for postproduction.

So far today, he'd kissed Mitzy Parker half a dozen times and still hadn't gotten it right.

"Cameron, you want a break?" Marshall asked, impatience edging his voice.

Noah scratched at the pancake makeup they'd had to apply to match continuity with the scenes shot before he'd spent two weeks in the high Montana sun. "I wouldn't blame Mitzy if she needed a break from me," he admitted ruefully.

Mitzy, busy puffing on her between-takes cigar, waved a hand in dismissal. Her motto was *Anything You Can Do, I Can Do, Too.*

"How 'bout ten?" Marshall decided, mopping his own forehead.

Cameron Ross was legendary for being the easiest actor in town to work with. It was unheard of to need more than three takes, unless the director was playing around. Noah knew that ever since he'd walked back in the studio, he'd been disassembling his good reputation at the speed of light.

But he couldn't keep his mind on the job at hand. All he could think about was a freckle-faced woman with cotton shirts and boot-cut jeans. Honesty and courage and the chance to end the subterfuge. He'd expected to think of windswept valleys and broad-shouldered mountains. He thought of constellations instead. Trumpet lessons and cows who walked backward.

He thought of a world-famous actor who was too chicken to tell the truth.

"Okay, ma'am, now you can go in."

"I told you it was an emergency, you idiot!"

Noah snapped to attention like a flag in a thunderstorm. He was on his feet so fast the rest of the crew stopped dead in their tracks.

He was either hallucinating or in more trouble than he knew.

"Don't you take your phone calls?" she was demanding as she stormed past two security guards and the AD, like Carrie Nation searching for a saloon.

Come on, Campbell, Noah goaded himself, faced with a female intruder on full steam. Say something. Protect yourself. Protect the lie you've worked so hard to set up your entire adult life.

"I'm talking to you," she persisted, planting herself not two feet from him, security guards trailing in her wake like ineffectual satellites.

"Do you know her, Mr. Ross?" one asked, reaching for his gun.

The other one tried to grab her arm. "She said . . ."

She shook him off like a bug.

"No," Noah demurred, hand up, eyes on his visitor. "It's okay. She's . . ."

"His cousin, Sally," she said, still focused entirely on Noah.

Sally.

Sally, who recited gossip magazines like poetry, who could name the birthdate and shoe size of every celebrity in Hollywood. Who had drooled over the pictures of Cameron Ross in his kitchen.

Who was supposed to be at least twelve hundred miles away at this very minute.

"What are you doing here?" he demanded instinctively.

Sally planted herself close enough to him to exclude everybody else on the set, even Mitzy Parker, who was the hottest ingenue to hit town since Julia Roberts.

"You and I need to talk," she said. "Now."

Noah didn't bother to say a word to anybody. He just grabbed her hand and headed for his trailer.

"Now, what's going on?" he demanded, shutting the door behind them.

Sally took a quick look around the Spartan furnishings. "I kind of expected more," she admitted.

"How did you get here?" Noah demanded. "How'd you know who I was?"

That actually got a laugh out of her as she dropped a purse the size of a trash bag on one of the chairs. "Every woman in the valley's known who you were since the moment you pulled Miss Retta out on the dance floor."

Noah found he was having trouble closing his mouth. "But . . . but you didn't say anything."

Sally scowled now. "You didn't shut down the roads, either. You just lived there like one of us. Counts for something."

Noah opened his mouth to ask the next question. The most important question.

"Yes," Sally accused, before he even had the chance. "She knows. But I guess it just didn't occur to you that that kind of thing doesn't mean anything to Dulcy."

Noah sat down, hard. All that fear, all that worry and work. All for nothing.

All so he could sit here and wonder just what the hell Dulcy had seen in him, anyway.

"She knew."

Sally shrugged. "She figured it out. I think you could have given her a little credit, movie star."

"Yeah." He dropped his gaze to his hands that were suddenly so restless. "I guess I should."

"Ask me again what I'm doing here."

Noah lifted his attention right back to her. "What *are* you doing here?"

That quickly her expression changed. She started pacing, which in a trailer that size wasn't comfortable. "Ethan," she said. "He was going to get in touch with you and let you know."

"He didn't."

"You told them to hold your calls."

Noah waved off the truth. He'd been trying to escape several persistent agents and a producer, who knew he was back in town. All he'd wanted to do was this week of work and then get the hell back to the ranch to finish sorting things out. To clear things up with Dulcy.

Sally's hands were clenched. Her cheeks, usually so pink, were pale. "Noah," she said. "We need your help."

"Dulcy," he said, somehow knowing.

Sally dragged in a breath. "She's been kidnapped."

# Twelve

Noah found himself back on his feet. "What are you talking about?"

Sally grabbed her purse and riffled around in it. "I have a copy of the note. They want money from you."

"Money? What are you talking about? Haven't you gone to the police?"

"Bart's waiting for us to call. I got here as quick as I could."

Noah didn't know what to do. He was shaking. Ever since he'd skyrocketed to fame after his third film, he'd lived with the chance of somebody trying to take advantage of that. He'd had his share of stalkers, a petty thief or two.

But this.

Dulcy.

"What happened?"

Sally was still elbow-deep in her purse, her attention on what she'd brought. "She left a message for Ethan that somebody had taken Hannah—"

Noah's heart stopped.

"Hannah?"

"She's okay. She's fine. Turns out she was out at a mall with Mom and Dad, and a couple of clowns got her to make the phone call."

"What clowns?" Noah demanded.

Sally looked up, smiled a tight little smile. "Clowns," she admitted. "With white face, big floppy shoes and all. At the food court at the mall. Bart thinks they'd been waiting for a public place. They didn't want Hannah, they just needed her to scare her mother. She did. Dulcy told Ethan she was heading up to meet the kidnappers on the north ridge. Colorado showed up later in the afternoon at the Lazy V with a note attached to his saddle."

The note Sally finally handed over.

"You have to help us," she begged. "We knew you'd know what to do."

Noah blinked at her, still struggling to come to grips with the news. "Me? Why should I know what to do?"

"Because you always do," she said simply.

That brought Noah to a dead stop. "Cameron Ross always does," he retorted. "I'm not Cameron Ross."

Sally didn't look in the least impressed. "That's the name on the trailer."

"I've also played three cops and an ambassador, Sally. It doesn't mean I can negotiate treaties."

She waved at the paper he held in his hand. "Read it. It's a copy I made."

Noah didn't know what else to do. He read the note. It simply stated that Dulcy was being held for a three-quarters-of-a-million-dollar ransom, payable in the usual small, unmarked, nonsequential bills. It also said that since Dulcy was so important to Noah, the note writer knew Noah wouldn't do anything stupid like contact the police or FBI, since the whole valley would know about it within ten minutes.

Which the whole valley would.

Noah. The note said Noah.

He looked up at Sally. "Does the grapevine know what happened between Dulcy and me?"

Sally snorted. "Why do you think she left?"

Noah found himself staring all over again. "Left? What the hell are you talking about?"

It was Sally's turn to sit. "Oh, hell. I should have guessed."

"Left? When did she leave? Why didn't I know?"

"One thing at a time here, Noah. The note. What should we do?"

"Call the FBI." He stopped. Thought. Fought his way through the sudden, searing terror at the idea of something happening to Dulcy to work out the logic problem. "No. The kidnappers would know. We can't do that. You said the women in town figured out who I was."

"Within about fifteen seconds."

"What about the men?"

Sally shrugged. "It's kind of been our little secret. After all, the men are all so worried about outsiders, you know. They might not understand."

Noah waved the letter at her. "In that case, it's one of the men behind this."

"We don't have much time, Noah. You're supposed to be at the ranch this afternoon to take their phone call."

He tried so hard to think. To know what to do to help Dulcy. It was so ridiculous. He was a movie actor, not a cop. A pretender. A fake. And yet Sally was watching him as if she didn't doubt for a second that he was going to be able to somehow save Dulcy.

"They want me to make the payment," he said, checking the note. That quickly he picked up the phone and dialed his cousin.

"Where the hell have you been?" Ethan demanded without preamble.

"Sally just got to me. Fill me in."

Ethan sighed, a tight, impatient sound that betrayed how attached he'd also grown to Dulcy. "Nothing else on the kidnapping. Bart Bixby's holding off on everything until he hears from you. He has one finger on the FBI's number and the other on the county helicopter's. Nobody else knows but us and the new manager, Hank something."

"That's something else you and I are going to have to get into," Noah retorted, not caring in the least how upset he sounded.

"It was Dulcy's idea, Noah. She didn't want to worry you. She figured she'd have better luck finding out what was going on away from the ranch, and take the heat off you at the same time.''

"She did, did she?''

"It worked, too.''

"What do you mean?''

"It's a little complicated.''

"All right. First of all, do we have the money?''

"Your bank in L.A. has it ready for you to pick up.''

A little of the tension seeped away. Noah wasn't in the least worried about the money. He was terrified that no matter what he did, Dulcy wouldn't get out alive.

"All right, who is it?''

"She's a genius, Noah,'' his cousin said. "Don't lose her.''

All Noah could do was close his eyes against the sudden pain.

"You know a Cletus Wilson?'' Ethan asked.

"Yeah. He's on my west side. He might have taken some of my cattle.''

"He also bid on your ranch. Not only that, but there's a rumor going around town that he's got a filly on the side. Somebody who's costing him some money.''

"Like money from my account?''

"Hear this out. Dulcy went to see the wife. There is no girl-friend. No unexplained absences, no funny behavior. Cletus spends twenty-four hours a day trying to keep his ranch running. He's having problems, too. Now, on a different subject, there was a company called International Investment Trust that tried to buy the Lazy V. Do you know Barry Feldman and Jack Logan?''

"Yeah. Jack has a place there. I saw Barry in town visiting him.''

"They're partners. They tried to buy Cletus's place when they tried to buy yours, and Cletus's is right next to Logan's.''

"And?''

"And surveyors were up there yesterday deciding where would be a good place to put ski runs.''

"On property they don't own.''

"Uh-huh. Guess what bank they're going through?''

"Oh, God. Not First Montana.''

"On the nose.''

"So Bob Grumman, Feldman and Logan are trying to buy up property to build a ski resort?"

"Looks like. Only you and Cletus wouldn't sell."

Noah's mind was working a hundred miles a minute. "Sally," he said, turning on her where she was trying to make sense of the one-sided phone call. "Does Cletus Wilson keep anybody in his line shack in the summer?"

"No. We're only doing it at your place because of the rustling. He hasn't had any problem."

Noah's heart was beating faster. "Then that's where they have Dulcy."

"You want me to tell Bixby?" Ethan asked.

"No. No." Noah calculated, considered. Thought about how devious the plan was, how intricate. He decided in that moment exactly what he had to do. "You need to do a few things for me, Ethan. First, run the bank's records one more time for me. There are a couple of accounts I need checked, see if Bart can get the subpoena to do it. Double-check those against the list of IIT investors. After that, get your butt on a plane," he demanded. "Sally and I will meet you in Bozeman in five hours, no later."

"Me? Why me?"

"To play me, of course."

"What the hell are you talking about?"

"We're going to catch us some kidnappers, cousin."

Please let this work. Please, God, let this work.

Noah had been chanting the plea like a litany all the way from Los Angeles to Bozeman on the Beechcraft. From Bozeman to the ranch by the back roads where nobody would see him. From there across more backroads, farther down the valley.

It had to work. He couldn't consider anything else. He especially couldn't consider how ridiculous this all was, with him running in like the action hero he wasn't. He'd left Marshall gasping in outrage and his agent screaming at earshattering pitch. And then he'd climbed on his plane and headed north to save the damsel in distress.

He couldn't do it.

He had to.

Somehow.

It was a gorgeous day, sunny and windy with the clouds dancing along the peaks and the grass shimmering like silk in the wind. It was everything he had worked for all these years. It tasted like ashes in his mouth.

"Noah, hello. Thought you'd gone back to Philadelphia."

Noah looked at the bland, surprised face that greeted him at the front door of the old ranch house and thought what this would do to Dulcy.

"I imagine you didn't expect to see me," he said.

Especially since Ethan had accepted the call not five minutes earlier at the phone booth by the laundromat to tell him where to place the money, and was even now very visibly on his way to do it.

"What . . . um, what can I do for you?"

Noah didn't answer. He just pulled his gun.

His host looked as if he'd been electrocuted. "What the hell . . . ?"

"I know" was all Noah said, trying so very hard to keep his voice even. To keep his manner calm, so that no one else in earshot would know what was going on. "I know all about IIT and the resort. I know that you've been trying to get Dulcy pushed out, and I know why. I also know that you're trying to frame Cletus Wilson for what's going on at the Lazy V. I can just imagine what people would think if I paid out all this money to get Dulcy back, and she was found later dead on Cletus's ranch, especially since the money won't ever be recovered. She is alive, isn't she? I think you'd better tell me she's alive."

The other man looked from the Glock automatic to Noah's eyes, where he would find no mercy. "What are you . . . what do you mean? Of course Dulcy's alive. She's staying in the Red Lion Inn in town."

Noah took a step closer. Vented some of his rage. He'd played a variety of this scene once, and the reviews had talked about how frightening he'd been. How convincing. Noah realized now how little he'd known about real rage. Real terror-born fury that spills out of you with a heat that could melt iron.

He knew now. "No," he said. "She's not. She's up in Cletus Wilson's summer pasture with two of your men."

"That's ridiculous! I'm calling the—"

He never got the chance to finish the sentence. Not with the barrel of a gun wedged between his teeth.

"You won't call anybody. Because if you do, if you do *anything* that could hurt Dulcy, I'll kill you." Noah leaned in a little, so that he could feel teeth grate against the metal. So he could smell fear erupt on skin. "Do you understand?"

The nod was minimal.

Noah nodded back. Pulled the gun back. "Good. Let's go."

"Why did I know you'd be involved?" Dulcy asked, trying so hard to be calm.

Josh glared at her from four feet away where he was pointing his gun at her nose. "I couldn't pass up the opportunity," he admitted. "Just wish I'd been in it from the beginning."

"And what's your mother going to think?"

"Screw my mother. The minute we hear that that money's picked up, I get the pleasure of shooting you right in the face if I want." He thought about it a moment, his gun bobbing a little as he mused. "Or maybe I'll strangle you. Or bury you alive. Yeah, I like that. What do you think, Bill?"

The other man in the little cabin didn't bother to look away from the window. "Yeah, sure. Works for me."

Dulcy fought down the revulsion and took her own look outside to where the sun was beginning to set again. "The day you have the guts to shoot somebody in the face is the day pigs fly."

One look at Josh proved that she should have kept her mouth shut. Dulcy should have known better. She had to keep quiet. Be passive, cooperative. She had to get away from here alive.

Hannah was waiting for her. Noah.

Oh, Noah. This sure wasn't what you had in mind when you decided to settle in Montana.

"I don't suppose I could go outside and use the facilities," Dulcy asked.

She was sore. She was hot. She was stiff from sitting on this chair with her arms tied behind her back. Mostly, she was scared.

No, not scared. Blind, sweating, terrified. Even knowing it was Josh who carried the gun. Even figuring him for a coward. Dulcy had a feeling the other guy wasn't a coward at all. He just looked hard.

"Forget it," Josh said, still considering her. "Although if you're really nice, I might entertain you before I kill you."

Dulcy couldn't help it. "You've been watching too much Rambo, Josh."

"What the hell's he doin' here?" Bill demanded from the window.

Dulcy tried to look, too. She saw an old truck bumping over the high meadow, the kind of ranch truck that was endemic in Montana. A truck that looked like a hundred other trucks, a truck that was dented and battered and had the logo for the owner's ranch on the side.

The Triple M.

Dulcy's first instinct was to pull at the ropes. To try somehow and get out the door to warn Uncle Mike away.

Her second was to wonder why the two men were simply watching him approach.

Like they weren't surprised.

"Isn't he supposed to call?" Josh asked.

Dulcy's heart hit the floor. No, no, no. This didn't make sense at all. Not Uncle Mike. That weasel Bob Grumman, maybe. The outsiders with their impression of Montana as nothing more than a cash cow. Not Uncle Mike, who'd been born there and lived there.

The truck stopped outside, and the door opened.

"Guess he got impatient. Or something's wrong."

Josh snorted. "Great."

Dulcy struggled to see better. She wanted to see that it really was her Uncle Mike stepping out of the truck. Looking up at the cabin as if he were walking toward a scaffold.

Please—no Uncle Mike.

Bill walked to the front door and opened it. "What's going on?"

"You need to, uh, bring the girl here."

Dulcy felt something crawl along her arms. Prescience, like the feel of electricity right before the lightning was going to strike.

Bill didn't move. In fact, he looked around, to the old, grimy window at the side of the house, through the matching square that revealed Uncle Mike, standing all alone out there with nothing but the high meadow behind him.

"What's wrong?" Bill demanded.

Uncle Mike didn't answer. He looked toward the side of the house. Dulcy came straight to her feet, chair and all.

"Somethin's wrong," Bill muttered.

Dulcy pulled herself free of the chair just about the same moment he turned back to her.

"Bring her here!" Uncle Mike yelled again, his voice higher, thinner. Afraid.

Dulcy wanted to run. To barrel through the door. She could see the realization hit Bill that they were cornered. She knew he was going to need a hostage to get out, and she knew who that hostage was going to be.

She decided to barrel through Bill instead. Lowering her head, she dived right for his chest.

He bellowed. Josh charged in to help. Dulcy yelled, exhilarated by the feeling of that soft whoosh against her head. She felt Bill go over and lost her balance. Josh came right behind, his gun up. Yelling obscenities at her.

Dulcy hit the floor, and all hell broke loose. The side window exploded, and Dulcy saw somebody somersaulting in through it. She heard gunfire, so close to her head that she tried to curl up in a protective ball. She felt the cold nudge of a gun barrel against her temple and went still.

"Let her go!" came the harsh, terrible cry, closer than the gunshots. "Let her go let her go let her go!"

A huge, frightening sound that she finally recognized as Noah's voice.

Noah.

Dulcy tried to lift her head, to see him. She saw hair and denim that belonged to her captor. She thought she saw Noah alongside, his gun grinding against the head of her captor. She thought there were more people, but she couldn't tell. She was deaf and caught and fighting for breath.

"I'll kill her!" Bill holding her screamed back, right in her ear.

"And then I'll kill you, you bastard. I'll blow your eyes out and then your knees and then your freakin' nuts! Let her go!"

"Let her go, man!" Josh screamed from a little bit away. "It ain't worth it!"

But Bill yanked Dulcy to her feet instead. "I'm gettin' out."

Dulcy saw Noah then. She saw those gentle eyes go flat and dark and deadly. She saw him lift a gun in a steady two-hand grip that followed Bill to his feet. She saw Noah rise along with him, a terrifying figure of fury.

She was afraid. Of him. For him. She wanted to reach out and soothe him. She wanted to plead with him not to do something foolish. She wanted to fold into his arms and let his gentleness loose again.

"I'll give you five seconds," he told Bill through clenched teeth. "Five."

Behind him, Bart had Josh in an arm lock. Uncle Mike stood like a puppet in the doorway, and some other men circled outside. But Bill wouldn't notice. He would only see Noah. He would only see the madness that glittered in those stone-hard gray eyes. He would only know that Noah was giving him no choice at all.

"Noah, settle down," Bart pleaded.

Dulcy couldn't take her eyes off the man she'd thought she'd known so well. She couldn't seem to stand on her own or stop shaking.

"Four."

His voice was getting softer, deadlier.

Dulcy didn't want him to shoot this man. She didn't want to see the madness take root there where only bright smiles should live.

"You don't have the guts," Bill challenged, his own voice shrill and trembling.

"Three."

Dulcy did the only thing she could think of. She dropped.

Bill stumbled with her sudden weight. The gun slipped, and she spun away. Six people sprang into action at the same time, and Dulcy thought it was over.

She thought that until the first gun went off. Until the second one followed within seconds and exploded in her face.

# Thirteen

"**D**ulcy!"

She was deaf. She thought she might have been blind, and the side of her neck felt as if it was on fire. Even so, she tried to get up. To get to Noah.

"Dulcy, are you all right?"

She blinked, trying to see through the stinging powder from the close-range shot. "I'm okay, Noah. I'm okay."

She tried to get to her feet, but her knees wouldn't cooperate. She needed to get to Noah. He had his gun back in Bill's face. He had his other hand around Bill's throat. Bill was gurgling, struggling to get in air.

"It's okay now," Bart assured everybody as he handed Josh off to somebody else. "Everybody back away."

Noah wasn't listening. He was still intent on a struggling Bill.

"Noah," Bart repeated. "It's over. I'll take him now."

Noah didn't pay any attention.

Dulcy finally made it to her feet. She stumbled over to where Noah was silently, ferociously squeezing the life from her captor.

"Noah," she begged, struggling against the ropes that kept her hands from him. "Noah, stop!"

His attention wavered, dropped. He seemed to really notice her for the first time.

She did her best to smile. "Please," she begged him, her voice quiet. "Give him to Bart. Let's go home."

His eyes widened. Dulcy could see that his hands were starting to shake. His face, so tanned and handsome just a few days ago, was the color of putty.

He sobbed with relief. "I thought . . ."

"I know. It's all right now."

He let go. Bill slumped almost to the ground, gasping and gagging, before Bart hauled him out the door along with the gun Noah had shoved against his head.

"Are you really okay?" Noah asked, his trembling hands up to her face, to her hair. His own face was bleeding from half a dozen small cuts on his forehead. His chest was heaving, and there was sweat pooled under his arms. Dulcy couldn't stop smiling.

"I'm really okay," she promised. "I could use a hand with these stupid ropes, though."

He couldn't manage the knots. He was shaking too badly; he was too impatient. Finally Bart did the honors and stepped away just in time to keep from being included in an embrace.

More than an embrace. A completion, a possession, the two of them coming together as if reuniting a broken whole.

Dulcy gave in to another sob, thankful to just touch Noah. To know he was there. That he was safe and whole and in the same room.

It was enough.

It didn't seem it was enough for Noah. He wrapped his arms around her, bent his head over her, until she couldn't see or hear anyone else around.

"You scared me," he admitted on a whisper.

Dulcy closed her eyes against the exquisite sense of comfort. The reassurance of his heartbeat against her ear, his callused hands in her hair.

It couldn't last. She'd known that since she'd begun to suspect that those blue eyes hadn't been a figment of her imagination after all. Since that night she'd heard him call Marshall

Wellman a bastard for making him spend more time with Mitzy Parker.

For this brief moment in Noah's arms, it didn't matter.

"You really did it," she said, still shaking pretty badly herself. "I knew you would."

Noah straightened enough to glower down at her, his eyes still preternaturally bright. "You, too? What do I have to do to convince people that this isn't me?"

Dulcy folded herself into his arms and smiled. "It isn't, huh? Then who came crashing through that window?"

He ran a trembling hand through her hair. "I decided I had to get in the quickest way possible," he said, defending himself. "Especially when I saw you do your fullback impression at that big guy."

"The big guy you almost throttled to death?"

His answer, when it came, sounded more surprised than chagrined. "Yeah. I guess I did."

"You should have seen him at your Uncle Mike's house," Bart offered from the doorway. "Amazing."

"Necessary" was all Noah would offer.

"I guess it just proves that you deserved that Oscar after all," Dulcy teased, her eyes closed and her attention mostly on the feel of his racing heart, of the soft cotton of his shirt against that hard, strong chest. "You scared the hell out of me."

"Nobody was acting today, Dulcy," he admitted, his cheek against her forehead, his arms so tight round her she could hardly breathe. "I was terrified."

"Ready to go, Sheriff?" came a familiar voice from the door.

Dulcy opened her eyes again and peaked around Noah's shoulder to find Paco standing in the doorway with Hank. Behind them were the rest of the hands, all cradling Winchesters and grinning a bit sheepishly.

"*You* were the posse?" Dulcy asked, touched by their presence.

"You bet," Billy Boy admitted. "We didn't get you back, we'd have to keep workin' for Hank here. Didn't suit us, ya know?"

Even Hank was grinning.

For once in her life Dulcy wished there was more she could say than thank you. "Thank you," she said, anyway, knowing they'd understand.

They did. Chuckling and jostling like kids, they all retreated out beyond the cabin to leave Dulcy and Noah alone. Dulcy heard the rest of the people sorting themselves out for the ride back down the mountain and ignored them. She only focused on Noah. On knowing that he was all right, on knowing that she meant enough to him for him to do what he had this evening.

"I'm sorry."

"For what?" Noah demanded. "Solving the problem? Ending up on the wrong end of an extortion scheme?"

"Making you worry."

"I doubt sincerely this is going to be the last time you do that, Dulce," he admitted.

"I was never once kidnapped until I met you," she protested. "Contrary to popular opinion, I also don't seek out much excitement in my life."

Dulcy had meant to be flip, funny. The minute she said it, she knew she'd made a mistake. It wasn't much of a reaction, but it was there, deep in his eyes where she'd learned to look.

"I guess this is where I should say I'm sorry, too," he apologized, his own grin not as easy. "I should have trusted you with the truth about who I was."

Dulcy made it a point to flash him a completely irreverent grin. "Now, this is a discussion I think we've had before."

He smiled for her, and Dulcy thought maybe it could be okay. "I've never had anybody prefer gray eyes before," he admitted, his eyes briefly, baldly vulnerable. Shy. The honorable, hardworking man Dulcy had grown to know in this valley, before she'd realized what his place was out in the real world.

The real Noah Campbell she'd fallen in love with.

"We don't trust flashy people in this valley," she teased. "We're just ranchers here, ya know."

"We need to talk."

"Oh, yes, we do," she agreed. "But first we need to get home. I need to see Hannah, and you might just need some stitches. You're bleeding."

He didn't bother to reach up to the cut along his hairline. "Real windows are a lot harder than candy glass," he admitted.

"I imagine. Looks like it hurts."

"No." Now his expression grew rueful. He still didn't move. "My ankle hurts."

Dulcy looked down to see that he really wasn't putting any weight on his left leg. "Your ankle? What happened?"

He grinned, but his heart wasn't in it. "I think I broke it when I came through the window."

Dulcy couldn't help it. After all that had happened in the last few hours, in the last days and weeks, all she could do was laugh. "I guess you're right after all."

"About what?" He didn't seem nearly as amused.

"I've never heard of Cameron Ross doing something that dumb. You must be Noah Campbell after all."

Good thing, too, because it was Noah Campbell Dulcy wanted to kiss. It was Noah Campbell who kissed her, deeply and sweetly and thoroughly. It was Noah Campbell who let her help him out to the Jeep and down the mountain. It was Noah Campbell who asked her to come home with him to the ranch with Hannah when the work of the night was all over. It was Noah Campbell she accepted.

"So let me get this straight," Hannah said. "Clowns are strangers, too?"

"Yes," both Dulcy and Noah answered in unison.

"Even in the circus?"

"Especially in the circus," Noah offered.

Dulcy ignored him. "Unless I'm with you, they are," she assured the little girl.

Hannah spent a few minutes nodding to herself. "Okay. Can we come back now, Mom?"

Dulcy didn't answer right away. She hadn't gotten that far yet. It had been enough to get back down from that line shack to find Hannah entertaining Noah's cousin Ethan on the porch of the ranch house, and from there include those two and Sally in the ride to take Noah to Bozeman to get his ankle X-rayed and casted.

Noah had used the ride time to explain how he'd figured Uncle Mike to be the only local devious and hungry enough to be the silent partner in IIT. How, once they'd gone in with the court order, they'd found Uncle Mike's accounts to be in far worse shape than anyone in the valley had thought. In bad enough shape that being the enforcer for a huge buy out had made sense to him.

Uncle Mike had not only known that Cletus Wilson couldn't have financially stood the suspicions they'd cast on him, he'd known better than anyone in the valley that Dulcy was the secret behind the Lazy V's success. Without her, he felt he could systematically wreak havoc until Noah decided to quit the valley, and IIT could move in uncontested.

Uncle Mike had not only underestimated Noah, but Dulcy, as well.

"Of course you're coming back," Noah assured Hannah from where he lounged, leg propped on a pillow, on the couch.

Seated on the floor alongside with Hannah in her lap, Dulcy looked up to shoot him a cautionary glance. "Noah and I still have to talk about that," she demurred.

"You have to come back," Ethan objected from his spot on the recliner, the almost-as-handsome twin of his more famous cousin. "Hank won't talk to me."

"Hank won't talk to anybody," Hannah informed him.

"Hannah and I haven't finished our Hootie Hoedown yet," Noah objected to Dulcy. "You can't go."

"Don't I hear the bedtime bell?" Sally interjected from her own spot in the rocker.

"Aunt Sally, I just got home," Hannah protested.

Sally was already on her feet. "Well, you can make sure nobody's snuck in and redecorated your bedroom. Come on."

"Mo-o-om."

Dulcy gave Hannah a little push in the right direction and followed to her own feet. "Aunt Sally's right, honey. Come on. I'll tuck you in."

"Check the room for any suspicious clowns while you're at it," Noah suggested.

Hannah groaned. Then she leaned over and dropped a kiss on his cheek. "Thank you for bringing my mom home."

Noah grinned. "It was my pleasure, Hannah."

Dulcy took Hannah's hand and led her on upstairs, Sally's voice following her up.

"So, is Mitzy Parker as wild as I've heard?"

It didn't take Dulcy long, but by the time she got back, both Sally and Ethan were missing. There was just Noah, stretched out on her couch like a movie diva, his hair tousled and his jaw just showing new stubble. Now that it was a moot point, he'd left out his gray contacts. His eyes were blue. Bright, blinding blue, the color of morning glories. His force field hadn't dimmed any, either, licking along the surface of Dulcy's limbs and setting up a dance in her chest that robbed her breath.

"Strategic withdrawal, huh?" she asked, bending to pick up half-drained glasses.

"Ethan drove Sally home."

Dulcy nodded, skittish, wondering how this story was going to be retold, since Sally's car had been sitting out in the driveway right alongside the truck they'd probably taken.

"Hope he doesn't get lost," she said, straightening.

As she walked by, Noah grabbed her wrist.

"Sit down," he commanded gently.

Suddenly, Dulcy felt fidgety and shy. "I need to..."

"You need to talk to me," he said.

She did. She knew it. So she set the glasses back down and settled herself alongside him on the couch. And she tried, very hard, to look into those blue eyes. To ignore the sudden flash of memory that put her back in his arms, tangled in the sheets on a stormy afternoon.

"The moment of truth," she blurted out, trying very hard to be flip.

Noah reached up and drew a finger along her cheek. "You know that discussion I was going to have with you when I got back?"

"Uh-huh."

"I have a question."

Dulcy wanted to back away. She couldn't seem to separate from his touch, though. It wasn't just electricity. It was life. A surging thrill of the world that seemed to seek her out and infect her whenever she was with him. A different, more visceral awareness she hadn't allowed herself since it had hurt her the last time.

It was Noah. Hard-edged and soft-eyed and as much a part of her now as Hannah, as Montana, as breathing.

"The answer is yes," she said very quietly. "A person can fall in love in only a week."

For a second it seemed the light had drained right out of Noah's eyes. Dulcy held her breath, unable to take back what she'd said, unable to go on. Terrified of the lightning in those startling blue eyes and even more terrified of losing it again.

"And now," Noah said. "Is it any... different?"

"You mean because you're also Cameron Ross?"

"Yes."

She considered him. Considered how different he was with his smooth cheeks and blue eyes, how she never would have been comfortable with him if he'd shown up like this the first day. She tried very hard to consider implications, complications.

"Yes," she said honestly. "It is."

He seemed to actually deflate before her eyes. Dulcy couldn't tolerate it. She knew, suddenly, what his question had meant. What he needed from her.

What she could give, because she'd never meant anything more in her life. Because no one deserved it more than he.

"I fell in love with Noah Campbell," she said, unable to keep her hands away from him anymore. "And that's who I'll always love. Who I'll always want. I have no idea how I'll get along with Cameron Ross."

"Could you, though?"

Dulcy actually managed a chuckle. "Can Cameron Ross get along with me?" she asked.

Noah smiled back. "Cameron Ross couldn't keep his mind on the movie he was shooting. He kept thinking of this spitfire redhead in Montana."

Dulcy's heart rate kicked up. Her chest seemed suddenly tight, as the spark flared between them. Was it her imagination that Noah's heart seemed to speed up as well beneath her fingers? Did his pupils widen, just a little?

A man couldn't lie with a physical reaction like that, could he?

"He did?"

Noah wrapped his hands around hers, held them gently against the hard warmth of his chest. Reconnected them both to what they had felt and been and known. "I know this isn't an easy proposition," he said. "I've been thinking of it, though. Actually, I've been thinking of it so much I haven't gotten anything else done."

Dulcy grinned right past the breathlessness, the sudden, exhilarating uncertainty. "Which was why Marshall Wellman was screaming over the phone an hour ago."

"Well," Noah admitted with that wonderful, brash grin of his. "That and the broken ankle. I'm screwing up his shooting schedule."

"To save little old me?" she asked with a wide blink to her eyes.

His grin faded, and his grasp tightened. "I'm serious, Dulcy. I've never been more serious in my life. Will you hear me out?"

Finally, no retreat, no games, no jokes. "Yes," Dulcy agreed. "I'll hear you out."

He nodded, arming himself, she thought, with his certainty. His need. "You belong here, Dulcy. In Montana, on the ranch, with your family and friends. And even though I'd have to leave for long periods of time to film, I want this to be my home. For you to be my home. Do you think you could live like that?"

"And Hannah?" she asked.

"Are you kidding?" he demanded, his smile a rare gem. "I already bought her a harp."

Dulcy stopped breathing altogether. "You did?"

"Do you think she'd be interested in the proposition?"

"I don't know," Dulcy admitted. "It's something we'll have to work through, the three of us."

"And you wouldn't mind my only being here part-time, just like before?"

"I think the cat's out of the bag about who you are," she said.

"Yeah, but on the other side of that, the valley's sure decided they made a mistake. You'll have all the help you need."

It was true. As they'd stopped back at the sheriff's office to finish making statements, she and Noah had been met by a veritable procession of townspeople who had professed their apologies. More had left food on the doorstep, like high cholesterol penance. It seemed that Dulcy's attempt to save the valley from the grasp of outside developers had offset her reputation. Even her Aunt Mary hadn't been able to really fault Dulcy for her part in Uncle Mike's downfall.

And Noah? Noah was a knight in shining armor in the finest tradition of the Old West. Noah had saved not only one of their own, but the valley itself. Instead of a poor, benighted fool, he was now considered an honorable, brave man. Noah was one of theirs.

"Well," Dulcy demurred, struggling to maintain a straight face when she felt like flying. "I wouldn't really want to uproot Hannah right now and look for a new job."

Noah let go of one of her hands to reach for her hair tie. "It would be traumatic," he agreed, his concentration on pulling it out. Pulling her braid out with it so her hair tumbled over her shoulders.

Dulcy struggled to keep from groaning at the sudden shower of chills he was unleashing. "And I've just got the breeding program in shape."

He pulled her close until his lips were against her ear. "Best in the state."

Dulcy opened her mouth to answer. She couldn't manage words. He was nibbling at her earlobe and winnowing his hand in her hair. He was somehow managing to free the buttons on her shirt at the same time. Dulcy shuddered, closed her eyes, felt herself sinking right into that fire that seemed to spark and flare from his fingers, from his tongue. From the smell and sound and touch of him against her.

"You're gonna hurt yourself," she gasped, knowing she should pull away. Arching against him instead so he could find her breasts. So he could torment them with his newly callused hands.

"I already did." He chuckled against her hair, granting her wish. Slipping his hand inside her plain plaid shirt, inside her serviceable bra as if it were a seductress's lure. Wrapping his long fingers around her breast and letting his thumb torment her nipple. "Thought it was time to feel better."

Dulcy gasped again, writhed against him. She could feel him hard against her and thought if he could forget the cast on his leg, so could she.

She had more to say, she knew it. She couldn't remember what it was, suddenly. She just knew she wanted her clothes off in this hot house. She wanted her skin abraded by rough hands and the hair on a man's chest. She wanted to rub against him, curl around him, watch those blue eyes get all dark and smoldering as she tormented him.

"You haven't given an answer yet," he protested as she let her own hand wander. As she undid buttons she needed freed and examined a badly strained zipper.

"You're distracting me," she answered agreeably, moving carefully alongside him. Splaying her hand against his chest and thinking that it was a magnificent chest, a heck of a set of shoulders, a pair of thighs that begged exploration. Moving already so that she could accommodate him, so she could give his hands free rein.

Dulcy lost her shirt. She helped Noah out of his. She undid zippers and flies and got her own boots off so she could straddle him. So she could torment him with her mouth and her hair and her soft skin. So she could know that he needed her as much as she needed him.

He did. He groaned. He bucked. He held on to her as if she were saving him from a long fall. He whispered her name and then groaned it. He held her with his hands and delighted her with his mouth, her hair falling over them both like a fiery cascade, her hips moving, already undulating against his hand, against his clever fingers, against his murmured urgings.

They were balanced on the couch, trying to protect his cast, his jeans half-off, her clothes strewn across the floor. It didn't matter. Only they mattered, what they needed, what they had missed, what they so wanted to promise. They promised with their hands and their mouths and their bodies, and when Dulcy lowered herself onto him, they moved as one, faster, faster, their smiles growing as they feasted on each other's eyes, on each other's smiles, on the sweet fire they'd never found anywhere but on this couch, in this house, in each other's arms. They sang and spun and laughed, until they climaxed almost together, their heads back, their hands tight, their bodies sweat sheened and satisfied. And then, shattered, they sank into silence.

"You still," Noah managed to say sometime later, still not moving, his arms around Dulcy, "haven't answered."

Dulcy knew she should move. He was probably awfully uncomfortable. It didn't seem to matter. "Mmmmm," she murmured. "Let me get this straight. You here for six weeks at a time, all the time. Kind of like being with a traveling salesman who travels all at once."

"Kind of like. Except you have one thing wrong."

"Oh?" She knew he could feel her heart stumble with sudden, stupid fear. "What's that?"

"That 'being with' part. I don't want you to 'be with' anybody. I want you to marry me."

That was what got her to push up off his chest. "Marry?" she asked, as if she'd never heard the word before.

She would have thought he was lying except for his eyes. "Marry. Like for better or for worse. All that."

He meant it. Dulcy could see it. She believed it now, which was just doing worse things to her heart rate. To her throat, which seemed suddenly full of tears.

"I would like to at least meet Cameron Ross a time or two before I make up my mind," she managed to say, trying so hard to maintain any sense at all, when all she could think of was waking up alongside Noah every morning.

He held on more tightly. "You'll try?"

Dulcy straightened, her hair brushing the tops of her breasts. She faced those unnerving blue eyes and thought that they really were the same—warm and inviting and just a little uncertain. They were Noah's eyes, and she would promise them anything. Give them anything.

"On one condition," she said, anyway.

Noah never hesitated. "Anything."

"That when you're here, you don't shave."

That stopped him cold. "Why?"

She smiled and gave in to the impulse to winnow her hands through his hair. "Because Noah Campbell doesn't like to shave, of course. Or dress up. He wears battered jeans and a hat that's put out one too many fires, and he loves Hootie and the Blowfish. He rides like a cowboy and curses like a sailor and loves more than anything when he can wade around in the mud and manure and work his ranch.''

Dulcy saw his uncertainty explode into joy and felt it echo in her chest. In her heart. In the deepest recesses of her, where for so long she had been so careful not to court it.

"That's the only you I want, Noah," she told him. "It's the only you I need."

"It's going to be a lot to put up with," Noah cautioned.

Dulcy laughed. "Hannah's going to go through puberty in about five years," she reminded him. "*That's* going to be a lot to put up with."

"I'm not perfect."

"I'm the one who dragged you in here the first night. You're not telling me a thing."

He held on tighter. "You mean it? You'd like to try?"

"I mean it, Noah."

His eyes. His sweet, searing eyes that had always compelled her. Now they seduced her, his eyes and nothing more. Dulcy saw in them everything she could have wanted, more than she could have dreamed.

"I love you, Dulcy," he whispered.

Dulcy didn't know how to feel more. Her heart battered at her chest, and her throat ached with the sweetness of his words, with the incandescent flame of his eyes.

He loved her. He loved *her*. Even after touching ground back in his other life where the women didn't have to scrape cow manure off their boots, where he could have anyone or anything he wanted.

He wanted her.

Dulcy smiled, knowing Noah saw the tears in her eyes. "I love you, too, Noah."

"Not Cameron?"

"Cameron doesn't live here," she said, lifting his hand and placing it against her heart. "Noah does."

"Then I'm home," he marveled softly. "I'm really home."

Dulcy smiled. "You're home."

Bending over, she proceeded to prove it in the simplest way she knew. And even with his leg in a cast, both of them battered and bruised and exhausted, they found their home together in each other's hearts, in each other's arms. In the sweet, throaty music of their laughter that drifted out on the night breeze to where the Montana night arced high and silent over a huge old Victorian house and the new family nestled inside.

# Epilogue

It was magic. Perched on the edge of a beautiful summer night, Los Angeles glittered like a gaudy treasure. Spotlights snaked across the sky, and traffic edged closer to the theater, where a crowd of over a thousand waited. In a city that had increasingly moved toward a casual attitude in dealing with world premiers, this one was a throwback, tuxes and sequins and limos. Cameron Ross was introducing his new movie and his new wife on the same evening.

"You're sure about this," Dulcy said from where she watched the approaching crowd through the smoked glass of the limo.

Noah nuzzled her neck just beneath the fall of hair she and Sally had precariously pinned into place. "Absolutely. The quicker you get out there and let everybody see you, the quicker they'll lose interest."

Dulcy wasn't sure what was worse. The butterflies in the pit of her stomach or the shivers of need Noah was unleashing with his greedy mouth.

She knew which she'd preferred.

"I don't have to do this except at premiers and big things," she reminded him. "Right?"

He had found her earlobe. "Right."

"The rest of the time I can stay happily on the ranch with Hannah and everybody."

"Right."

The limo stopped and the driver stepped out of his door. Dulcy could see the crowd turn away from the sashaying Mitzy Parker to see who was going to step out of the limo.

"Noah, I can't do this," she protested.

Noah finally lifted himself away from sampling her neck to smile for her. Not a Cameron Ross smile, all gloss and no substance. A Noah smile, the kind he saved for her and Hannah and Sally. The kind that lit his eyes like summer lakes and stole her heart all over again.

"I can't believe this," he protested. "You, Dulcy McCann, telling me you can't do something? I thought that wasn't in your lexicon."

"Dulcy McCann Campbell, if you please," she objected. "And if you think that in my lifetime I ever envisioned this one, you're nuts. I'm a ranch hand, Noah. Not a model."

Noah took a second to tuck a wayward curl behind her ear. "You're my wife. You're funny and brilliant and sensible, and I love you enough to stay in this limo and drive it straight back to Montana if you want." He considered her hard. "Do you want to?"

She considered him in his Armani tux and his collarless shirt, his suave, silky good looks and startling, mesmerizing blue eyes. The other Noah, she called him. The dark side, Noah called himself. She should have been bowled over by the sight of him, the smell of him, the feel of his smooth cheek against her hand.

She liked the real Noah better.

But this one would do in a pinch.

Then she looked down at the simple black silk sheath she wore, adorned with nothing but her wedding band and diamond stud earrings Noah had given her for their third anniversary. The important anniversary. They'd been married for two months. They had known each other nine, which, with Noah's traveling and filming schedule had translated into about three they'd shared in the same spot. It hadn't mattered. They had done all right apart and celebrated like randy teens when they'd gotten back together. Not a traditional relationship, certainly, but one that was increasingly comfortable. One Hannah had finally endorsed by writing the Campbell Wedding trumpet concerto. One the valley had signaled its approval of by protecting Dulcy while Noah was away and including them both when he was home.

"I don't belong here," Dulcy insisted again.

"Neither do I," Noah assured her. "But if we don't let them know, they'll never figure it out."

Alongside Noah, the door opened silently. Dulcy could hear the rising roar from the audience, the scattered intros from the interviewers.

". . . new wife, Dulcy, whom he met while on vacation last year. We're going to get a word with them now. . . ."

Dulcy stoked herself one more time on her husband's smile. "All right," she agreed. "We'll go in. But just so you're facing this as off balance as I am," she said. "I want you to know something."

Noah was already stepping out of the car and couldn't turn back. The crowd outside howled, screamed, jostled. The TV interviewers pressed closer to catch the moment when they would all be treated to the first sight of the new Mrs. Cameron Ross.

Noah uncurled from the limo and straightened. Gave his tux a small settling yank and turned back to hand Dulcy out of the limo.

"What do you want me to know?" he asked, so that the sound men couldn't hear him.

Heck, Dulcy almost couldn't hear him. Flashes were strobing as she put a foot on the pavement. Sound ricocheted along the street. Somewhere Sally and Hannah and Bart were already inside the theater, where they could watch without being bothered. Dulcy could hardly breathe, but she did it. Took Noah's hand and stepped out of the car with all the grace Sally had taught her. She smiled for Noah. For the cameras that blinded her. She turned to her husband and let him have it.

"Congratulations," she said. "You're going to be a daddy."

The next day Sally made it a point to tape the "Entertainment Tonight" episode that recorded the moment when Cameron Ross, the new Cary Grant, the embodiment of grace and sophistication, tripped in front of the world and fell right on his face.

*  *  *  *  *

## FORTUNE'S Children™

Bestselling Author
# LISA
# JACKSON

Continues the twelve-book series—FORTUNE'S CHILDREN
in August 1996 with Book Two

# THE MILLIONAIRE AND THE COWGIRL

When playboy millionaire Kyle Fortune inherited a Wyoming
ranch from his grandmother, he never expected to come
face-to-face with Samantha Rawlings, the willful woman
he'd never forgotten...and the daughter he'd never known.
Although Kyle enjoyed his jet-setting life-style, Samantha and
Caitlyn made him yearn for hearth and home.

MEET THE FORTUNES—a family whose legacy is greater than
riches. Because where there's a will...there's a *wedding!*

*A CASTING CALL TO
ALL FORTUNE'S CHILDREN FANS!*
If you are truly one of the fortunate
few, you may win a trip to
Los Angeles to audition for
Wheel of Fortune®. Look for
details in all retail Fortune's Children titles!

Look us up on-line at: http://www.romance.net

FC-2-C-R

# Take 4 bestselling love stories FREE

## Plus get a FREE surprise gift!

**You can run, but you cannot hide...from love.**

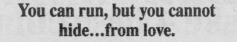

This August, experience danger, excitement and love on the run with three couples thrown together by life-threatening circumstances.

Enjoy three complete stories by some of your favorite authors—all in one special collection!

**THE PRINCESS AND THE PEA**
by Kathleen Korbel

**IN SAFEKEEPING**
by Naomi Horton

**FUGITIVE**
by Emilie Richards

Available this August wherever books are sold.